The King of Claddagh

by

THOMAS FITZPATRICK

Abridged by
UNA MORRISSY

THE MERCIER PRESS
CORK

The Mercier Press Limited
Cork
25 Lower Abbey Street, Dublin 1

ISBN 978 1 78117 902 4

Transferred to Digital Print-on-Demand in 2024

CONTENTS

.

ONE

The Buff-Coat Minister

A bright, calm afternoon towards the end of April, 1652, had been suddenly darkened by a drizzling bank of fog drifting in over Galway Bay from the Atlantic. The sound of the rushing Corrib waters mingled with the screams of the sea-birds. To these were added now and then the unnerving cries of human beings in grief and anguish. They came from boats putting off from the Galway side, which could be seen only dimly through the haze by those on the western shore.

What could be going on? The question was being discussed by little groups of men in odd but distinctive attire who had collected in front of the thatched cabins on the bank, called from its situation on the river, the Claddagh. To be sure, holding such little palavers was their sole occupation when they were not out fishing. But anyone accustomed to their habits would have noticed that there was something apprehensive in their attitude, as they talked earnestly and quietly, heads together, hands thrust into side pockets.

As a rule what was going on in the town held no interest for them. There was so little communication between the two peoples that no Claddagh man ever crossed the great West Bridge except on urgent business, and few had ever as much as seen the East Gate. They differed in dress, taste, occupation and wealth. They even looked different.

The people on the east side, the town side, were tall and mostly fair, with a somewhat haughty bearing. The inhabitants of the Claddagh were short, hardy, dark-haired and dark-complexioned; conscious of being the older race, and quite unheeding of the *Gaillimhe*. No two peoples living a thousand miles apart could have differed more widely: the one a Firbolgian tribe by whom Ireland was originally colonised, the other an Anglo-Norman colony, mere 'new-comers' who could claim an ancestry of only four hundred years.

From the town side of the river came now and then the shrill note of the trumpet or the beat of a drum, and the keen eyes of the fishermen could discern the figures of Roundhead soldiers pacing the river wall. Then a boat appeared off Renmore Point bringing three people towards the Claddagh. As it scraped in upon the strand there was a general movement towards it, as if important news were expected.

Two of the boat's occupants were fishermen; the third, though dressed like them, seemed different. He was taller, and his fine, full beard marked him out as a rather uncommon Claddagh man. Moreover all the men touched their caps as he approached.

In the forefront of the little group was a man beyond middle age, of square, solid build whose fine, silver-haired head and unmistakable air of authority singled him out from the rest, though he was as simply dressed as they were. He was Conor MacRigh, the King of Claddagh and Admiral of the herring-fleet plying between the coast of Iar-Connacht and the shores of Burren and Corcomroe.

'What news do you bring, Father Anthony?' asked the King of Claddagh respectfully of the bearded man.

Father Anthony's tidings were that the new military governor of Galway, Colonel Peter Stubberd, had led a raiding party on the previous night through the country between Roscam and the river at Claregalway. The soldiers had seized a large number of people as they fled their homes, and had put them all, regardless of sex or condition, aboard a ship which was to sail when the fog lifted for the West Indies, where they would be sold as slaves to the sugar planters.

This grim news was received with murmurs of sympathy, and of anger at *Sasanach* treachery. Only a few days

6

previously several ships had left the bay carrying Irish soldiers who had been permitted to join the Spanish and other Continental armies in accordance with agreements made by the new Parliamentary commanders. To have followed the departure of the soldiers with a raid upon the now disarmed peasantry was in breach of their word, and a sinister sign of what to expect from Cromwellian rule.

'It's a sad enough sort of time for a wedding, Maeve,' observed Father Anthony compassionately to a beautiful, dark-eyed young woman with rich, dark hair, who had just come out of a cabin. She wore the simple dress with the red petticoat of any fisherman's daughter, though it was her father who ruled the Claddagh. Of the two young men who had been in the boat with Father Anthony, one was her brother Cahal and the other Carbra Conneely whom she was going to marry.

A strident voice sounded suddenly from the ruins of the Dominican friary, and the bulky and uncouth figure of a Cromwellian soldier bore down towards the cabins, bearing a huge book on the flyleaf of which was scrawled in an ignorant hand, 'john mathews his Bible'.

He stopped about thirty yards away, holding the book aloft. 'See how the Lord smileth on his chosen people,' he bellowed, waving towards the town; then pointing to the little cabins and the ruined friary he went on, 'and see how he smiteth them that know him not.'

He prated on in this strain, but his message was lost on the Claddagh people for no one understood a word he said, and they stared in astonishment at his gestures.

'That's Mathews,' Father Anthony told them in Irish. 'The weaver-soldier who has just taken possession of Menlough Castle. He wants to "convert" us. Let him alone. Neither heed nor hinder him.'

Just at that moment word was brought to the King of Claddagh that soldiers under the command of two mounted officers were crossing the West Bridge. It was clear that they were coming to the Claddagh, and the soldier-preacher, as if he had been expecting them, hurried back and held a conference with one of the officers.

The villagers fled, disappearing not into their cabins but over the western crest and into a maze of passages leading to numerous islets beyond the Claddagh. Meanwhile from the east side, where there was a large stretch of treacherous slob land, the second officer was approaching the Claddagh. In pursuit of some of the fugitives, who knew the ground well and escaped, he galloped into the dangerous bog and his horse began to plunge so violently that the rider was flung head downwards into deep mud. His head and shoulders were sunk in the semi-liquid morass and there he would have suffocated but for the help of two men in fisherman garb who went to his rescue. His own troop, busy searching the little cabins, knew nothing of his plight.

He seemed almost insensible when the two men pulled him out.

'Is he dead, Father?' asked the younger man.

The older signed to him not to address him as 'Father' even in Irish, as the officer opened his eyes and stared with the puzzled gaze of one awakening from a trance.

'Tell me, sir,' said the old man, as he helped the officer to sit up, 'what does all this mean?'

The officer looked at him, somewhat surprised to hear English well spoken by someone dressed as a Claddagh fisherman.

'It is all a mistake, I think,' he replied in some embarrassment. 'Colonel Stubberd thought arms were concealed in these hovels. Pious Jack Mathews, I fancy, led him to believe that you were brewing mischief, so we got orders to take hostages for your good behaviour.'

'You expected to find weapons among poor Claddagh fishermen? I assure you there is not and never has been any such thing in our possession. If you choose, I will help you to search.'

The officer thanked him and said he had no wish to pry into the cabins but would look to his horse, which had struggled to higher ground and was awaiting him.

'I owe you a debt of gratitude,' he said, remounting. 'You will find that Major Charleton is not the man to ignore such generosity where it has been so little deserved.'

At that moment Carbra Conneely came running towards them to say that his beloved Maeve, her father, brother and many more had been carried across the West Bridge by the *Sasanach* soldiers.

Distraught he raised his hands to the Major and implored him to free them. He spoke only in his own language, but the Major, rightly interpreting his pleas, promised to do what he could to help the poor people so unjustifiably torn from their homes, though he warned that others might have more influence with the Governor than he.

He cantered away towards the West Bridge which at this period was guarded by three gates, one at each end and one in the middle, and all protected by guard-towers against the possibility of surprise from Iar-Connacht.

The prisoners had already been brought into the town and awaited the decision of the Governor. The Major gave his mount to an orderly who stabled it with the rest of the officers' horses, in the fourteenth century church of Saint Nicholas. He was immediately accosted by the sanctimonious Mathews, who was rejoicing at the outcome of his 'mission' to the Claddagh.

'Where are the prisoners?' cut in Charleton coldly.

'Where the Governor ordered,' replied Mathews. 'There is to be a council meeting in an hour to seek assistance from the Lord for dealing with this stiff-necked people.' He would have ranted on, but the Major, who had no time for Mathews' arrogant belief that he had the right to preach to all and sundry, walked away and left him standing.

9

TWO

The Cromwellian Council

When Charleton had washed and changed into a clean uniform he went to the courtyard of the Governor's house where the Claddagh captives were being detained, among them the King, his daughter Maeve and his son Cahal.

In the centre of the courtyard stood the Governor, Colonel Stubberd, and some members of his staff and council.

'Did they find any arms?' Lieutenant-Colonel Hurd asked the Governor.

'Only these,' said a non-commissioned officer producing a couple of boat-hooks.

'Fool!' roared the Governor. 'What do we want with them; or indeed with some of these savages you brought in? They wouldn't be worth their freight to the plantations. Let me see your face,' he said to Maeve, who was clinging to her father holding her apron up before her eyes. 'I forgot; this pretty savage does not understand any civilised language.' He turned to a local citizen of Galway named Lynch Fitz-Thomas who was now serving the Roundheads. 'Who is she?' he asked, 'and who is that man to whom she is clinging?'

'It is the King of Claddagh, so please your worship,' translated Fitz-Thomas.

'King! A king still within these dominions? He shall have shorter shrift than Charles Stuart! Ah, here comes Major Charleton. Why, Charleton, I was afraid you had fallen into the hands of the Philistines.'

'I was more fortunate,' returned the Major. 'I fell in with

Christians.'

Don't let Mathews hear you say so,' said the Governor laughing; and leaving the prisoners under guard he and the other officers went into the house to hold their council.

The meeting was not harmonious. Leading fanatics like Mathews and Camell urged that the Claddagh captives be immediately put aboard the ship for the West Indies. Charleton and the Eyres among others opposed this; while Paul Dod, Brock and others waited to see what the Governor might think.

Mathews then launched out into an account of how he had opened his bible that morning and found a passage urging him to destroy all the Lord's enemies. This was the work of the Lord, he insisted.

'And cursed are they who do that work negligently,' added the less talkative but no less fanatical John Camell.

'And who, pray, will be your hewers of wood and drawers of water?' demanded Charleton. 'Why do you twist Holy Writ for the authority to slay or banish people who have done you no wrong? These poor fishermen have not made war on you. They have not even made common cause with your adversaries. It is all very well for you, Mathews, to pursue the people who have lost by our coming here. You have been given the Castle and lands of the Blakes of Menlough. But whoever else might threaten your possession of them it is not these men. I would further submit that if you banish all the people who have been supplying Galway with food you will bring famine upon us. It is not wise to have this town at the mercy of foreign supplies.'

'You make some good points, Charleton,' commented the Governor. 'I shall think the matter over at leisure. Meantime I think I may free the older captives.'

'And the women?'

'Pardon a moment, Charleton. I forgot. What did I hear about a King? The Parliament and people of England will have no king.'

11

They will hardly behead a king who dresses, lives and eats like the poorest fisherman in the hamlet,' returned Charleton. 'He is, moreover, a king who claims no authority except what is given to him by the free voice of his people, people whom he advises rather than rules.'

'In that case,' said the Governor, 'he may be allowed to follow his craft, provided he does not in any way help our enemies.'

The Governor's decision caused some murmuring, Mathews and Camell in particular thinking it not only dangerous but sinful to reprieve these 'heretics'.

In his heart the Governor despised these canting fanatics. But he could not ignore them for they stood high in the favour of the Lord President of Connacht, Sir Charles Coote, and also of the Commissioners for the Affairs of Ireland, back in Dublin.

Charleton pressed for the release of all the prisoners taken that day, but the Governor did not care to go wholly against Mathews and Camell, who were real bigots. He himself was a bigot only because bigotry was in the ascendant and profitable, and Stubberd was above all things greedy. He had some soldierly qualities, and left to himself he would not be cruel for the sake of cruelty. What he did, he did for gain.

He refused, therefore, to release the women that evening, and poor Maeve and some half-dozen other young women were detained while Conor MacRigh and other older people were freed.

It was a sad night for the King of Claddagh. His darling Maeve had not returned, nor his son Cahal. He heard that Cahal and the younger men had been sent to the Lion's Tower, the strongest of the fourteen towers on the town wall, but he knew nothing of the fate of Maeve and the other women. Fearing that they were to be put aboard the ship bound for the West Indies he and a faithful friend spent the night in his boat to make sure that Maeve and his other dear people were not taken to the prison-ship. But the ship sailed before sunrise and no more prisoners had been sent out to it.

A ray of hope glimmered faintly through the clouds of the King's many sorrows. His wife and one of his children had been mortally wounded during the infamous buccaneering raid on the Claddagh ten years ago, and his little home and belongings reduced to ashes like most of the others. His eldest son had gone to sea against his father's wishes and was believed lost for no word of him had ever been heard. Another son, Donough, had also left home, for he was thinking of the priesthood. And now the hope of his declining years, Maeve and Cahal, were perhaps about to be consigned to a terrible fate, while his intended son-in-law Carbra Conneely had been arrested at the West Bridge where he had gone to seek news of Maeve and her brother.

THREE

'An Aristocracy in Hovels'

Charleton was fond of boating, and on the morning following the raid on the Claddagh he was walking on the river wall when he noticed a boat being pulled upstream by a single oarsman. Hailing it he climbed aboard and found himself in the company of the English-speaking boatman who had saved his life.

Both were pleased; Charleton at finding a boatman to whom he could talk, and to whom he owed a debt of gratitude, and the boatman because he had met the very man he wished to see in the hope of learning something about the prisoners.

Charleton's news was scanty but startling. Maeve and three other young women had been sent to the vacant house in Cross Street from which the nuns had been evicted by the Cromwellian soldiers. The women had been seen by the officer on guard at ten o'clock the night before; at six in the morning when the guard was changed they had vanished.

No trace of them could be found, and nothing suspicious had happened during the night. The guard, in fact, had been doubled and the Governor himself had inspected it twice. The closest scrutiny of doors and windows, even of the roof and chimneys had yielded no clues, and so far as anyone could make out it was like witchcraft.

The boatman listened with interest rather than surprise.

'They are not gone in the ship to. . . ?'

'No, no,' replied Charleton. 'The party who wanted that were out-voted. I believe my argument carried some weight with the Governor. He may not be much influenced by humane considerations, but he has more practical sense than some of those around him. I think those poor women will be all right.'

'And the young men?'

'That I cannot say. But they can be thankful that the West Indian ship was allowed to sail without them.'

They were passing between Renmore Point on the east and Rintinane on the Claddagh side when an elderly man pulling a small fishing boat drew near them, a look of anxious enquiry on his face. Charleton's boatman waved to him and called out in Irish, 'All will be well; Maeve is safe.' He then pulled quickly away towards Hare Island to avoid attracting attention from the castle on Mutton Island, and the Major, who liked fishing, made a show of casting lines; but the real object of his trip was to learn from his boatman something about the strange people of the western bank of the Corrib.

'How did it happen,' he asked, 'that these people did not

learn civilisation from those on the eastern bank?'

'Learn from the people of Galway!' exclaimed the boatman. 'You know very little of the aristocracy of The West —as we term the Claddagh side.'

'Aristocracy!' cried the astonished Major. 'An aristocracy in hovels!'

'You have hit upon the correct description,' observed the boatman. 'The cabins are hovels. The people who inhabit them, however, have all the essential characteristics of ancient aristocracy—except wealth, and the many things good and bad which accompany it.'

Charleton was still puzzled. He allowed that the inhabitants of Galway might perhaps have claimed to be an aristocracy, but they had kept apart from the Claddagh and from all the Irish of Connacht.

'Rather say,' rejoined the boatman, 'that the Claddagh holds aloof from the *Gaillimhe*. On the West Bank we have a Firbolgian settlement of an antiquity which dwarfs the Norman. Such people would think it degrading to do as the *Gaillimhe* do.'

'How comes it that you, a man of English speech, can make yourself so much at home among the remnants of the Firbolgian nation?'

'That, too, I could explain,' replied the boatman, 'but it might not be prudent to enlighten a Cromwellian on so delicate a subject.'

'You cannot suppose me to be so degraded a monster as to take advantage of the man to whom I owe my life. You may speak in confidence, for I know you are no ordinary boatman.'

The matter of first importance for the moment, the boatman said, was whether anything could be done to rescue the prisoners from exile, or to set them free.

Charleton thought it possible that something might be achieved by an indirect approach to the Governor, though it would not be easy to obtain the freedom of men out of whom plenty of money might be made by sending them to the plantations.

'Do you know the tobacco merchant?' he asked the boatman somewhat casually.

'Stephen Deane? I do, well. He is my uncle.'

'Indeed! And his daughter?'

'Gertrude is my first cousin; and my god-daughter,' replied the boatman. 'I was her sponsor,' he went on, deciding to give proof of his trust in Charleton, 'just before I entered my novitiate, but I have seen little of her since I joined the Dominicans.'

He noticed that Charleton was interested in the Deanes and appeared pleased to have found someone so closely connected with them. He seemed to think, too, that it might be possible to work on the Governor through Mr Deane. Stubberd was said to have a part interest in a tobacco plantation in Virginia, and there was a fairly steady contact between the two men.

Deane, in fact, was just the man through whom a suitable arrangement might be made. He was the cool, calculating business man whose tongue and temper were well under control, all qualities which particularly recommended him to the money-loving Governor. For the present, Charleton thought, Deane seemed to be the only promising opening; and now he appeared eager to hear more about Deane's daughter.

'You have met Gertrude, I presume?' asked the boatman.

'The first, and almost the only time I met her,' replied Charleton, 'was while she was attending to one of our soldiers who was stricken with the plague. It had been in the house where he was billeted. She had been attending to the people of that house, and when she heard that a Cromwellian soldier had caught it she looked after him just as if he were one of her own.

'When I heard of her generosity and heroism I was deeply impressed, and I determined to meet her. When I did, I felt as if I were in the presence of a princess and not the daughter of an ordinary citizen in any Irish town.'

The boatman smiled at Charleton's obvious admiration for the girl.

'She was brought up by the Dominican nuns after her mother died,' he told him, 'and after she went home to live with her father she always visited them. That plague was the result of the terrible privations during the nine months' siege of Galway, and the convents were the hospitals to which the sick and wounded were brought. At first Gertrude worked with the nuns. Then she took her skill and experience into the people's homes. Even after the surrender she went on doing this work, but recently she has not been able to go out on her visits because of the behaviour of the soldiers on the streets.'

A flush of anger passed over Charleton's grave, handsome features.

'Thank you for telling me that,' he said. 'I will have enquiries made and see that a stop is put to such disgraceful conduct.'

As they rowed back Charleton asked if it would be possible for them to meet for excursions on the Bay or the lake whenever the weather was suitable. So it was arranged that Father Anthony, for of course he was the boatman, would be ready at stated times to act as the Major's official boatman.

'You have nothing to fear from me,' Charleton told him, 'though I cannot speak for others. You are known, of course, to many around the river?'

'To many of the poorer sort; and some on the town side would recognise me. But there is only one man, so far as I know, who might betray me.'

'You mean. . . ?'

'Marcus Lynch Fitz-Thomas.'

'That sneaking, detestable fellow! Believe me, you are in no danger of meeting him in my company. What name shall

I know you by?'

'Roe,' replied the 'boatman' with a smile, pointing to his auburn har. 'The word means red.'

Having landed his passenger the 'boatman' pulled a short way down the water, then shot across to a sort of cave or bight which contained a number of fishing boats. The sails hung loose to dry, all dark in colour except one which was white. As his boat entered the cave heads rose from every boat, and from under the white sail an anxious voice asked, 'have you any further news?'

'All will be well, with the help of God,' replied Father Anthony.

FOUR

Rivals

Returning to the Governor's house in High Street Charleton found that Colonel Stubberd was still in bed. He had, of course, been up most of the night and he was not one to neglect his comfort.

It occurred to Charleton then that he might make use of the time to begin the enquiry he had promised into the matter of the behaviour of soldiers on the street towards Miss Deane.

The tobacco merchant's premises fronted on to a different street but the back of it met up with the rear of the Governor's house, and there was actually a secret door through which they could communicate. Charleton himself had taken messages from Colonel Stubberd to Mr Deane by this route when it would not have been prudent for either man to be seen in the other's company.

The merchant was in his counting house, as he usually was except when he was asleep, and it was here that he had received Charleton on previous occasions when he came from the Governor.

'I come on my own account this time,' Charleton told him, 'and partly on your daughter's. I understand that the boorishness of certain individuals wearing the uniform of the Parliamentary Army has prevented her from carrying on her charitable work, and I would like to obtain some facts.'

Deane listened and then, suggesting that Charleton should meet Gertrude and hear what she had to say, brought the Major through into the house.

When Gertrude entered the room Charleton was struck once again by her beauty and dignity. They discussed the purpose of Charleton's visit, but she could not supply names nor identify anyone.

'Some drunken rowdies, perhaps,' put in Mr Deane.

'Yes,' agreed Charleton. 'Our discipline has been sadly relaxed since we entered the town. The wonder is that men can get drink where there has been such famine. Drink seems to be inexhaustible however scarce bread may be.'

At this point the merchant was called out to deal with someone who wished to speak to him, and it seemed to Charleton that Gertrude had grown suddenly more reserved. She probably felt little desire, he acknowledged to himself, to be communicative towards anyone who was part of the system which had brought such calamity on her town. Besides, she could hardly feel at ease with someone whose outlook she believed to be utterly hostile to her religious beliefs.

'I am afraid, Miss Deane,' he said after a long and awkward silence, 'that you must consider my visit an intrusion. You have little reason to place much reliance on a Roundhead soldier.'

'I am sure there are exceptions,' she answered.

'It may not be easy for you to credit any of us with fair

or honourable dealings. But permit me to say that if you will let me have particulars of any misconduct I shall not abuse your confidence.'

She told him briefly then of how when she had gone out on her visits drunken soldiers had pestered her; on one occasion one had snatched her purse, and while he was emptying it she had escaped. This kind of thing was becoming more common, and now her father would not hear of her going out.

Charleton suggested that if she would arrange to make visits at a fixed time he would have a guard sent out to arrest anyone attempting to interfere with her. He asked her to consider this idea and took his leave.

As he passed the counting house on his way back he was addressed rather familiarly by someone standing in the doorway. He turned to see who it was, then passed on without giving any recognition to the well-dressed man who spoke to him. It was Marcus Lynch Fitz-Thomas, trying to draw the Major into conversation, or, perhaps, reminding him that his visit was not so private as he might have thought.

'Fawning spaniel!' muttered Charleton as he unlocked the door back into the Governor's house.

Then he remembered hearing that Fitz-Thomas had ideas of marriage to Gertrude, and that though the young lady herself did not favour him her father considered him quite eligible.

'One thing I'm sure of,' said Charleton aloud, 'is that so high-spirited and fine a girl will never consent to be the wife of such a reptile.' Then he looked round in alarm in case his spoken thoughts might have been overheard.

Lynch Fitz-Thomas was a member of one of the oldest families in Galway, and by repute one of its wealthiest citizens. Here, however, rumour was wrong, but Fitz-Thomas did nothing to correct it. On the contrary, his vanity and love of show led him to put up a show of affluence which he did not possess.

During the nine months' siege of Galway he had wavered between the two parties into which the townspeople had so unhappily divided, and when neither gave him the importance he wanted, he entered into secret and traitorous correspondence with the Parliamentarians. After the surrender he ingratiated himself with the Governor and the leading Puritans, and the new rulers were happy to have such a convenient instrument to their hand.

Deane was not aware of the relationship between Fitz-Thomas and the Cromwellians. He thought it no more than the kind of business connection he himself had with the Governor. He saw him only as a prosperous young man, and though he was reluctant to part with Gertrude, he thought she would be safer, in the new and dangerous situation in Galway, if she were married to a reliable citizen.

He had spoken to her on the subject a few times and was dismayed to find that far from finding Fitz-Thomas acceptable she disliked him intensely. It had not occurred to his practical, business-like mind that his unworldly daughter should have a clearer insight into the man's character than he.

Deane had pointed out to Gertrude more than once that in these days of military licence she might be carried off by some Roundhead officer or soldier against her will. To this she had answered that as far as that danger was concerned she would trust in God; but that she would never willingly marry a man whose hands were red with the blood of her countrymen, or whose spirit was darkened by bigotry. And, she added, she would rather sell fish or do washing than live in opulence in some mansion from which the rightful owners had been driven by force.

Deane thought it advisable to refrain from urging his wishes upon her. He believed that such vehemence arose from her youth and inexperience, and would fade away sooner if he did not unwisely oppose her.

21

FIVE

A Mysterious Illness

The Governor did not rise from his bed that day, nor for
many a day and week afterwards.

A member of his household, who eventually entered his
room to enquire why he was so late in rising, found him
very ill, and apparently delirious, which created conster-
nation not only among his own staff but throughout the
Cromwellian garrison. There was no qualified Roundhead
physician in the town, and to call in a doctor from among
the 'natives' seemed a most desperate measure.

Some of them tried to convince themselves that Stubberd
was merely suffering from an 'excess' and that the effects
would soon wear off. But the more sensible believed, with
Charleton, that he was very seriously ill and needed a com-
petent doctor immediately, whoever it might be.

'Would you put the Governor in the hands of a Popish
recusant?' asked Mathews in horror.

'It is a medical man we require,' replied Charleton. 'The
Governor can have your spiritual help when he needs it.'

'You want to have him poisoned by a Jesuit in disguise?'

'No, Mathews. But neither do I want people to say that
you or I poisoned him.'

Mathews was silenced; and Charleton went out in search
of a physician.

Dr Athy who returned with him might have passed for a
Spaniard. He had been educated at Salamanca and Padua,
and had graduated with honours from both universities. His
dignified ease and courtly bearing never showed to greater

22

advantage than in the presence of the rugged Cromwellian soldiers through whom he had to force his way into the sick room.

After a short examination of the patient Dr Athy said quietly to Charleton, 'there is too much commotion in this room.'

'Is it serious, doctor?'

'I am afraid so. There is a danger of brain fever. Did anything happen to excite or annoy him? But first we must get these people to go.' Turning to the crowd he said, 'Gentlemen, it is absolutely necessary for you to go away, and to avoid the least movement likely to excite the patient.'

They all left, except Charleton who was asked by the doctor to remain. The two men pondered the matter for a while, but the Major was not aware of anything which could have caused such shock to the Governor's nerves or brain. The incidents of the previous day and night had indeed brought much shock to others, but to Stubberd they had meant nothing. To butcher a thousand innocent people would arouse no more compunction in him than gulping down a goblet of Spanish wine.

'It is strange,' commented Dr Athy. 'His condition points to only one cause, but we cannot look for an explanation until he begins to recover and can recall what happened. Now, who can attend him? These fellows in buff-coats are clumsy nurses. Is there anyone skilled here?'

'I know of none,' said Charleton. 'And none of us deserve much tenderness from your people.'

'Never mind that now. If you will undertake to maintain order and discipline in the house I may be able to get someone to nurse him. But these boisterious people must be kept out. I will leave my instructions in writing.'

In the sensation following the Governor's illness the case of the escaped women prisoners was forgotten, and if anyone did think of it he kept silent for it was expressly ordered by the doctor that no mention of it be made to the

Governor in case it had something to do with his collapse.

Contrary to general expectations, however, Dr Athy succeeded in bringing his patient through the crisis and restoring him to full health over a period of weeks, with the help of the nursing skill and care of Miss Deane and her maid, to whom Stubberd believed he owed his life, and of two nuns whose identity, for their own safety, was never disclosed to him.

One evening after the Governor had begun to improve the doctor and Charleton were discussing whether to allow certain people in to see him just to prove that all was going well when they were startled by loud, angry tones in the hall.

Charleton hurried downstairs. 'For God's sake, Mathews,' he remonstrated, 'control yourself. Do you want him to have a relapse?'

The doctor, following him, said firmly, 'Quietly, my friend, or go outside,' and he moved as though about to eject him.

Mathews, abashed, muttered an apology.

'Come this way,' said Charleton opening a door into a vacant room. 'Now, what is the matter?'

'While I was walking on my river terrace this afternoon,' spluttered Mathews, 'I looked down towards the town and the whole river as far as Tirellan was alive with boats tricked out with the gaudy allurements of Satan.'

'Indeed!'

'Then I saw them actually land on a portion of my demesne, so I sent my steward to order the heathenish creatures off and to warn them that if they remained fifteen minutes longer I would have the castle guard fire on them.'

'Ah!' said Dr Athy with a smile, 'I see what it was. The people of the town and country always used to gather in the grounds of Menlough Castle to celebrate May with various games and pastimes. The Blakes always made them welcome, and joined in the games as good neighbours.'

'You would not have one of the Elect follow the ungodly ways of the Blakes,' observed Charleton sarcastically, looking from Mathews to the doctor.

'It would be too much to expect,' returned the doctor with a sigh.

'But I am sure,' Mathews ranted on angrily, 'that I saw among that mob some of those women who were prisoners...'

The doctor, on his way back to his patient, turned in the doorway and raising a finger in rebuke stopped Mathews in mid-sentence.

'Mathews,' insisted Charleton as the doctor left, 'you must remember that we are all bound by Dr Athy's orders for the present, and just think how important is their purpose.'

*   *   *   *   *

On the landing outside the Colonel's room the doctor paused for a moment looking absently through the window when he suddenly noticed a pale, thoughtful face at an upper window in a house straight across the narrow street. Almost instantly the face disappeared.

'That face!' he murmured to himself. 'I ought to know it. I have seen it, but where?'

He was interrupted in his reverie by Major Charleton, who had come upstairs.

'Mathews has just told me that the men imprisoned in the Lion's Tower were removed early this morning to help repair the castle on Mutton Island, and that they will be kept there until it suits to sent them to the West Indies,' he reported.

'Maybe they will be just as happy to have some work to do,' said Dr Athy.

'How will the King of Claddagh feel, looking across towards them from their own home?'

Dr Athy then told the Major that he had decided to forbid visits to his patient for another week.

25

'Yes, I think that would be the best course,' agreed Charleton. 'That fellow Fitz-Thomas would have been in yesterday but for the sentry.'

'Let him wait!' said the doctor. 'Let them all wait a little longer, and then our responsibility will be less.'

SIX

Glimpses of History

During the siege of Galway, which lasted nine months, the inhabitants suffered every kind of privation while bravely repelling the besiegers, and yielded only when reduced to absolute want.

In the midst of the siege two desperate attempts were made to get supplies. About eighty of the inhabitants went out and seized a hundred cattle but were met by the enemy. Sixty of the people were killed and the cattle re-taken. Then two vessels laden with corn were pursued by two Parliamentary frigates; one was taken, one lost on the rocks near Aran.

Finally, wasted by famine and pestilence, the inhabitants submitted to a treaty of capitulation which was signed on 5 April 1652, by virtue of which the fortifications were to be delivered to Sir Charles Coote on 12 April; all persons within the town were to have life, liberty and six months to depart with their goods to any part of the kingdom or beyond the seas. Clergy were allowed the same time to quit. All were to have indemnity, except Dominic Kirwan and those who with him had—right back on 19 March 1641— captured the Parliamentary ship commanded by Captain Clarke.

The corporation charter and privileges were guaranteed. Sir Valentine Blake, Sir Oliver Ffrench, John Blake and Dominic Blake were to be delivered up as hostages. Coote was to procure ratification of this treaty within twenty days, and the new castle at Tirellan and the fort on Mutton Island were to be surrendered by noon on the day following the ratification.

Coote's despatches reached Dublin Castle at midnight on 11 April 1652, and even at that witching hour a council was called. The treaty was considered too favourable to the rebels. This decision of the council was despatched that night in order to prevent ratification, but the surrender had been completed by the time the messenger reached Galway.

On 12 April Colonel Peter Stubberd, who had been constituted military governor, marched into the town with two infantry companies.

It became clear from the first that the conquerors had no intention of adhering to the treaty. No sooner had the Cromwellians marched in than monasteries and convents were ransacked and, together with all the churches in the town, put to secular use. Altars and statues in St Nicholas's were torn down, and officers' horses stabled in the aisles.

A weekly contribution of £400 towards the garrison's support was imposed on what was left of the townspeople, and exacted every Saturday to the sound of trumpet or beat of drum which terrorised the inhabitants.

No wonder, then, that at the time of our story the inhabitants remained hidden in their houses. The streets were deserted except for a soldiery constantly intoxicated on either liquor or fanaticism, who alternately chanted hymns or hurled abuse at the 'tribes' as they called the old Galway families. People who had to go about their business did so at risk to their lives, and indeed no one could carry on any business without obtaining protection from someone in authority.

There was still a mayor and corporation, but they could

do little to defend an unarmed populace against military rulers, who acted on the principle that the inhabitants had no rights at all, and that even to allow them to continue living there was an act of too great 'mercy'.

These matters were being discussed one day in the Governor's quarters by Stubberd himself, now restored to health, and Mr Deane.

'There are people about me,' Stubberd was saying, 'who blame me for showing too much favour towards Popish recusants. I must move warily.'

'They cannot accuse you of showing more favour than the treaty allows. This weekly contribution, exacted by soldiers forcing their way into houses. . . '

'You need not mention the treaty, Stephen. It is only so much wasted parchment. I owe something to you, and a great deal to your daughter, and your house will not be ransacked if I can prevent it. But why don't people hand in their contributions at the beat of the drum, and then there would be no calling at houses?'

'In many cases they have no money.'

'Then they must pay in kind,' said Stubberd, tossing off a goblet of wine.

The same subject came up for discussion the following day between Charleton and Father Anthony, now disguised as the Major's boatman under the name of Roe, as they were pulling up river towards the great lake. As they entered the lower part of the lake they almost ran into a hooker in which were three men half hidden by a cargo of firewood. The man astern exchanged a nod with 'Roe'.

'You know that man?' asked Charleton.

The 'boatman' nodded.

'I've seen his face occasionally myself,' Charleton went on, 'at a broken window in the house opposite the Governor's. In fact the Governor ordered me to search it one day during his illness, but all I found there was a small stock of firewood and peat which a decrepit old fellow wanted to sell us.'

'Roe' explained that the principal supply of fuel for the town was brought down the lake and landed near the Abbey Gate. Then, in order to divert Charleton's attention from this particular woodman, he asked him why he thought the Cromwellians hated the Irish people.

'Has it ever struck you, as an Englishman,' he said, 'how closely connected is the hatred for our people with the love of our lands?'

'I have thought something of that kind since I came to this country,' replied Charleton. 'English zeal to civilise the Irish seems to me to be less important than English hunger for Irish land.'

'There you have it, Major! Did not the English proposal to civilise us amount to this, that we were to be exterminated?'

'You have almost stated the case of the Parliamentary campaign in Ireland, for it looks as though your devotion to Charles Stuart will cost you very dear. These are not my sentiments, but they are those of people in more important places. Of course not many of those who originally opposed Charles imagined where it would land them.'

'Not even Oliver?'

'Not even Oliver. He was most unwilling to come to Ireland at all. His idea was to make some arrangement with the Irish leaders and get back as soon as he could to watch the game in England. But the snatch victory over Ormonde at Rathmines changed all that.

'Instead, then, of making for Cork or Waterford, as intended, he landed at Ringsend. Drogheda and Wexford followed, and Oliver's stature grew rapidly. It was lucky for him that the King's cause was in the hands of such a wobbler as Ormonde, and that Ormonde found a new ally in the many-sided Inchiquin. There might have been a different story to tell if Oliver had begun at Clonmel where he almost met his match.'

'But what of the capitulation?'

'This much I can tell you: those who have been hostile are considered to have no rights whatever under any treaty. Besides, there are heavy liabilities to meet, and "the war must pay for itself", and you know what that means.'

As they approached Wood Quay on their return they saw an elegantly dressed man lounging near the landing place.

'Fitz-Thomas,' said the 'boatman'. 'I don't wish to meet him.'

'Neither do I,' said the Major. 'Pull in here and let me out.'

Fitz-Thomas made towards Charleton as he landed, but he brushed past him. The 'boatman' observed that Fitz-Thomas felt the snub, which was made more obvious by titters from a few bystanders, for he was disliked and distrusted by all sides.

Actually Fitz-Thomas was there to keep an eye on Charleton, for he believed him to be an obstacle between himself and Gertrude. To be sure Charleton had said nothing to make him think so; what was more, Gertrude was unlikely to favour a Roundhead officer whose political and religous outlook was so opposed to her own, a factor which Charleton himself appreciated very well.

But Fitz-Thomas was not the man to consider such things, and so he was keeping a close watch on his supposed rival.

SEVEN

The Problems of a Traitor

It was not from Charleton alone that the unprincipled Fitz-Thomas received rebuffs and contempt. The Roundheads in general distrusted him. The more fanatical among them looked upon him as a wily 'heathen' who simply wanted to defraud them. Others thought he might be useful because he knew so much about the ways of the Popish recusants. These made a show of being friendly, but even he knew that it was no more than a show.

His former associates made no secret of their dislike for his relationship with the Cromwellians, and soon he began to feel that the path of self-interest which he had chosen was leading him to very little happiness. But it was too late now, for he was well caught in the toils of the abler Cromwellians.

One of these, Paul Dod, congratulating him on his wisdom in supporting them, told him of a special job they had for him. They had decided in council, he said, to build a place of worship for themselves, and to make the inhabitants of Galway pay for it. It was the council's decree that Fitz-Thomas should now prepare a list of all recusants in town, and should fix the quota to be paid by each of them.

Fitz-Thomas, realising that he was in no position to refuse the commission, unpleasant though it was, made no objection. While they were speaking he suddenly noticed Mr Deane across the road, and leaving Dod, he went over to him.

'I would like to speak to you on a matter of importance,' he began.

'Pray, what is it?' asked Deane somewhat impatiently, for he had no wish to be seen by either Roundhead or *Gaillimhe* in the company of a man who was detested by both.

'I can help you,' said Fitz-Thomas importantly, 'if you will stand by me.' He then related what Dod had just told him, though he was careful to leave out the part he was to play in the scheme.

Deane looked as if he knew all about the matter already, including Fitz-Thomas's role.

'Is there anything more?' he asked, eager to get away.

31

'I can promise to keep you safe—if—you will give me—Gertrude...'

'I can't dispose of Gertrude's hand and heart as if she were a bale of merchandise,' said Deane emphatically. 'I was ready to favour you, so far as an affectionate father might, though I must say your activities recently have lowered my opinion of you. I am sorry,' he said, and he hurried away.

'You'll rue it!' cried Fitz-Thomas after him, 'and so will Gertrude.'

'Wasn't that Deane, the tobacco merchant?' enquired Dod who had crossed over to him. 'My friend Elijah Brock tells me that he is a man of substance, but on good terms with the Governor. He may even get the Governor to shield him...'

'Leave it with me and I may possibly...'

'If you can achieve anything your services will not be forgotten,' put in Camell who had now joined the pair.

'Camell,' said Dod, 'did you tell me that there are still some ministers of the heathenish religion lurking in the Galway region?'

'I said there is good reason to suspect that such dangerous persons may be concealed in or near the town. So now, Fitz-Thomas, there's an opening for you. If you can drag any of these troublesome creatures from their lairs you will do a good stroke of business for yourself, for Pym promised that not a priest would be left in Ireland.'

The wretched man immediately brought up all the difficulties involved in such a task. He knew very little; he had had practically no connections with such people; he would not recognise any of them in disguise. Moreoever, people who might help him in other matters would have nothing to do with such a mission. He was alone in his support of the Roundheads and such isolation exposed him to distrust from all sides. But it was all in vain.

'Come now, don't talk of difficulties,' warned Camell.

Then he went on to expound at some length on all the services Fitz-Thomas would have to render to the Cromwellians if he expected to keep their confidence. And it was made very clear to him that talking about the difficulties he might encounter would be no excuse for him if he failed in what he had been ordered to do.

EIGHT

The Traitor at Work

Whether Fitz-Thomas had any suspicion that the people he had been ordered to betray might be concealed in or near Deane's premises, or whether he was just seeking an excuse to be near Gertrude—who disliked him more every day—he took to hanging round Deane's house and store, attempting without success to see Gertrude, even if only at a window.

He toyed with the idea that if he got soldiers to search the place he might make a show of defending her from their insolence, but he rejected this as too desperate a course.

There were many abandoned and half-ruined houses in Galway, belonging to people who had fled the siege and did not dare return. One of these directly adjoined Deane's premises and he made use of the basement portion as a warehouse and packaging store, though he would of course return it to the owners should they come back. A man named Joyce looked after this department; he slept in a room there, and had his meals supplied from Deane's kitchen.

Fitz-Thomas decided to see if he could work through Joyce. He would be certain to know if any suspicious people were harboured in the premises, and if there were, thought Fitz-Thomas, he might be able to put extra pressure on Deane in respect of Gertrude.

But his plan failed. Joyce would have nothing whatsoever to do with him, heeding neither promises nor threats.

Then Fitz-Thomas demanded a contribution from him towards the building of the Puritan place of worship. This Joyce flatly refused. He had nothing except his weekly wage, he said, from which he was obliged to make a payment towards the upkeep of the army. It was cruel but it was not unheard-of in war. This new demand he would totally resist. He had nothing left to lose except his liberty or his life, and he would forfeit either before he would contribute anything.

Fitz-Thomas, seeing that he could get nowhere, consulted his Cromwellian friends, Dod and Brock, who immediately sent a party of soldiers armed with carbines to raid Deane's premises. They did not touch any of the goods but swarmed upstairs. On the first floor they found nothing, but at the top of the stairs leading to the second floor they came on a closed door. As they began to break it down with the stocks of their carbines they heard the shrieks of terrified women from within.

As they smashed the door down they were confronted by the figure of a beautiful girl whose great dark eyes flashed defiance as she stood with a drawn sabre pointed at the first man who attempted to enter. A soldier raised his carbine to fire at her, but the muzzle was suddenly knocked upward by the sword of an officer who had raced up the stairs in the nick of time. The ball lodged in the door-frame and the soldiers were instantly ordered down to the street. When the smoke cleared the officer saw, huddled in a corner, five or six women dressed as nuns while in the centre of the room, flushed but unawed, stood Maeve, daughter of the King of Claddagh.

'A brave girl!' said Major Charleton, for it was he who had come to the rescue, having followed the raiding party as soon as he discovered where they were going. Turning to the nuns he reassured them. 'I will protect you,' he said, and closing the door behind him he withdrew.

The malicious plan turned out to be a complete humiliation for Fitz-Thomas. Colonel Stubberd was furious when complaints were made to him by both Deane and the Major. He abused Fitz-Thomas and threatened to send him to the West Indies if he ever again interfered with Deane's premises without a proper warrant. Worst of all, from Fitz-Thomas's point of view, he had shattered his last hope of reconciliation with Gertrude through the influence of her father.

The following morning Charleton went out with his 'boatman'.

'Can't you do something to get these ladies to some place of refuge?' he asked Father Anthony. 'Believe me, it will soon be impossible to protect them in Galway. My power to help the defenceless is little enough, and it may get less.'

A Spanish wine ship was lying in the Roads at the time and the priest suggested that with the help of Conor Mac-Righ, the King of Claddagh, he might arrange to get the nuns aboard her. The difficulty would be to get them through the town.

'True,' agreed Charleton. 'The Government is willing enough to send your people out of the country, but I doubt that if these ladies were to be recognised they would be allowed to depart without at least serious insult.'

At dusk that evening Father Anthony and Conor Mac-Righ pulled their row-boat along the lee-side of Hare Island towards Ardfry, the beautifully situated home of Sir Richard Blake. As they drew in towards a landing stage at the back of the house they were challenged. Father Anthony's reply was sufficient and he went ashore leaving the King of Claddagh in the boat.

Sentinels were on duty as he sought an interview with Sir Richard, but after a short delay he was admitted and followed his host along a private path leading to gardens closed off and guarded by another sentry. Within these gardens were sheds which had recently been fitted up as a temporary home for some of the nuns driven from Galway by the Cromwellians.

Sir Richard had a town house, and it was to this that the nuns had originally gone for shelter, for as an influential burgess of Galway Sir Richard had believed that his property would be protected under the treaty of April, 1652. He was very quickly given to understand, however, that as a leading figure in the Confederation of Kilkenny he would not be permitted to remain in town or hold any property there. He removed his effects to Ardfry, and the nuns, in the guise of domestic servants, went with him.

Father Anthony's visit to Ardfry was to let Sir Richard know of the proposed plan for getting away to Spain all the nuns, including those under his protection, who would be willing to emigrate until the storm had passed.

Sir Richard, who would have done everything in his power to keep them safely in Ardfry, agreed that it could hardly be long before his property there met the same fate as Menlough, and that for the safety of the nuns the plan had better go forward.

NINE

Exiles

After sunset on the following evening a boat crept round Renmore Point, keeping close to the boulder-strewn shore to avoid attracting attention from the castle on Mutton Island.

Earlier in the day a number of women, each carrying a creel on her back and covered by the hooded cloak worn by countrywomen bringing butter and eggs and vegetables into the town, had passed through the North Gate. From there they took a roundabout route to the coast where they sheltered until they were taken off by the boat rowed by Father Anthony and the King.

'If we can just avoid being seen from the castle. . .' said Father Anthony.

But he had hardly spoken when a shot from the Island Fort struck so close to their stern that water was splashed into the boat spraying the passengers.

'Courage!' said Father Anthony. 'They have spotted us through their spy-glasses but we can baffle them.'

The King and he consulted together, then they turned the bow towards the natural causeway of shingle and gravel heaped up by the tide between Hare Island and the mainland. When the tide was out the country people used it as a roadway to cart seaweed, but at full tide it might be ten or twelve feet under water.

'The water is light on the bar,' said Father Anthony. 'We can get over—and then, just let them try to follow.'

The two oarsmen knew what the state of the tide would allow. They just cleared the ridge, causing a momentary sensation in the boat.

'Over!' cried the King of Claddagh. 'Now let them come!'

Coming they were, as fast as four lusty oarsmen could row, confident that they would soon overtake the heavily laden fugitive boat. MacRigh made for the Round Tower of Roscam so that the pursuers would follow direct instead of rounding the island to the south.

Sure enough the castle party fell into the trap. They made directly for the ridge and suddenly grounded, the crash being plainly heard by the refugees as their boat ploughed safely on.

'There they'll stick!' said MacRigh. 'Their boat is broken; though they can get out and wade if they have the wit to follow the ridge.'

Then altering his course the King brought his party to Ardfry without further interference. The Spanish vessel was not sailing for a few days, but the nuns would be safe at Ardfry.

Maeve MacRigh had gone there too with the nuns. It was not the first time she had met her father since the women had escaped, but she had never ventured to return to the Claddagh. The other women seized with her had long since gone back to their homes and no attempt had been made to recapture them, probably because no one could identify them, even though Mathews thought he had seen some of them at Menlough on May Day. But MacRigh's cabin had been repeatedly searched, and there could be little doubt that the object of these searches was his daughter.

The King of Claddagh had been happy to have Maeve thus evade the Roundheads, but the recent raid on Deane's premises had convinced him, and their friends, that she would not be safe either in Galway or Claddagh. She had become a great friend of Gertrude's, but regretfully Gertrude too agreed that she would be wiser to leave.

Maeve was not, however, going to Spain. She would be safer there, of course, but she would not leave her father nor Carbra Conneely who, with her brother Cahal, was still in prison. She was going to stay with a Mr Ffrench, an uncle of Gertrude's, who was on good terms with Colonel Stubberd as the result of an incident which took place some time previously. Returning home one evening Mr Ffrench came upon the Colonel who had become separated from his patrol and had ridden into a dangerous morass. In gratitude for his rescue Stubberd had promised Mr Ffrench and his family his continuing protection and he had shown no sign of breaking his word.

The King of Claddagh and Father Anthony remained at Ardfry until they had put the nuns safely aboard the Spanish ship. Then they accompanied Maeve to Tyrone House, Mr Ffrench's residence. The King was saddened at being separated, even though it was by only ten miles of water, from his daughter, but he was sensible enough to consider how much worse would be his grief if she were transported to the West Indies.

Both the King and Maeve believed that the two boys, Carbra Conneely and Cahal, were still imprisoned on Mutton Island, but Father Anthony knew differently. In fact they had been moved to a part of the Galway coast opposite Aranmore. There, with other prisoners, they had been put to building huts for a detachment of soldiers who were to be sent to invade the Aran Islands which had not yet surrendered. He knew, too, from Major Charleton, that when this work was finished the intention was to transport them, but both men considered it kinder to keep this unhappy knowledge to themselves for the time being.

After he had parted from Maeve the King of Claddagh returned sadly with Father Anthony to his desolate cabin. But the priest stayed a while to comfort him, and together they prayed for help and protection for their loved ones.

TEN

St Augustine's Day

On 28 August in that same year a great crowd of men, women and children gathered at the Holy Well at the foot of Fort Hill. The well is named from the Augustinian Abbey which once stood nearby. Mountjoy had built a fortress around the Abbey Church in 1602, but it was dismantled by the Confederates in 1643.

Just before the siege of Galway, 1651-52, St Augustine's Church on the east and St Mary's on the west were pulled down so that the Cromwellian forces would not be able to use them for their cannon batteries against the town, but it was understood that they would be rebuilt when the danger was over. However, the Cromwellians built a new fort near

Mountjoy's old one, and the Governor and his staff happened to be inspecting it when the gathering at St Augustine's Well attracted their attention.

'What does it mean?' asked Stubberd angrily.

'Some papistical mummery, I suppose,' replied Jarvis Hind.

'That cannot be allowed. The Lord-General and the Parliament of England will not tolerate the Mass. Lynch Fitz-Thomas, do you know what these savages are at, under the very shadow of our fort?'

With a somewhat cringing air Fitz-Thomas explained, 'they have come to pray at St Augustine's Well.'

'Saint-worship going on under our very eyes, and within a hundred yards of Cromwell's fort!' thundered Stubberd. 'Hind, call out the carabineers. Give these sick people some leaden pills!'

Screams and groans arose from the crowd as a volley from the fort sent them fleeing in all directions, some even rushing into the shallow waters of the Lough. To add to the panic the Governor gave orders to pursue and capture as many as possible.

Several people lay on the ground; others who had scrambled to their feet but were unable to run were seized as they vainly tried to hide among the ruined cabins or the great boulders near the well.

Major Charleton was ordered to take part in the pursuit. His colleagues knew that he disliked this kind of operation and resenting his attitude they determined to involve him in it. However it was fortunate for the hunted that he was sent after them, for he concerned himself with the wounded while many of those unhurt escaped. But a number of prisoners were taken while he went to the help of an elderly man who was in danger of suffocating in the water.

It was the King of Claddagh, who had made instinctively for the water, but had fallen, bleeding from a wound in the side, and would have drowned but for Charleton.

As the Major staunched the wound instead of hunting fugitives a group on the battlements drew Stubberd's attention to the fact that he seemed to be 'doing the Lord's work negligently', and Stubberd stormed over to him threatening to lock him up for neglect of duty. Charleton coolly replied that should the matter be reported to the Lord-Deputy he would explain his action. Stubberd said no more and turned his attention to the prisoners.

Charleton's first thought was to send the King back to the Claddagh by water but no boat was at hand. He decided then that he, and the other wounded, had better be brought into town where Dr Athy could see them. While the Major was considering how to move them Stubberd ordered him to guard them until carts came to move them to the citadel near the West Bridge, which he thought would be the best place.

'The best place!' exclaimed Charleton. 'It would be more chivalrous to shoot or sabre them here now. Sir,' he added, looking straight at the Governor, 'you are a soldier, and you are known for your bravery. Do you think today's performance becomes a soldier? It smacks more of those wretches who surround you. Surely there are men in the Council in Dublin who would repudiate today's action?'

'On the word of a soldier, Charleton, you touch a tender spot. When I see the helpless state of these savages. . . ! Very well. I'll hand them over to you to deal with.'

And so the King of Claddagh and the other wounded were brought to the house adjoining Deane's, and though the rooms were cheerless and dilapidated enough they thought themselves fortunate not to have been imprisoned in the citadel. In fact they were much blessed, for they had Dr Athy to attend to them and Gertrude to look after them. In addition Father Anthony called frequently, and Major Charleton kept an eye on their safety.

The King of Claddagh spoke constantly of Maeve, and Gertrude would have been inclined to send for her, but all her friends opposed the suggestion. It would be dangerous in itself, but there was another reason for keeping Maeve away just now.

A ship had left Galway for the West Indies. On board were most of the people taken prisoner on St Augustine's Day and she was expected to pick up those who had been building the huts opposite Aranmore. Maeve probably knew of the fate of her brother and fiance, but it was thought kinder to keep the knowlege from MacRigh for a little longer.

'How can anyone do the cruel things which Colonel Stubberd seems to delight in?' Gertrude asked Charleton one day when he called.

'I can say little in praise of him,' answered Charleton, 'but he is not wholly responsible. His worst crime is allowing himself to be influenced by Mathews, Camell and other fanatical wretches. They dun him constantly, suggesting what Sir Charles Coote would do if he were governor; and the curse of Cromwell is a benediction compared with the curse of Coote.'

'And these are the people with whom Major Charleton consorts!'

'True. But I can assure you, Miss Deane, that many a man who honestly opposed Charles Stuart would be delighted to part with such company if he could do so with honour and safety.'

'And profit?' put in Gertrude very quietly.

'Well, I have been thinking of retiring to the lands allotted to me on the border of Cork and Tipperary.'

'Where you would, surely, be haunted by the spirits of those robbed, perhaps even murdered, to make room for you! A soldier who would take such ill-gotten property I would look upon as a mercenary!' said Gertrude, as she swept from the room.

Charleton remained frozen to the spot until Dr Athy came in.

'Have you and Cousin Gertrude quarrelled?' he asked.

'No, we were discussing contemporary events.'

'I know her views,' said Dr Athy. 'Does she seem to you too severe?'

'No,' returned Charleton. 'As you perhaps know, I am myself unpopular because I dissent from the majority. The Governor acts on the advice of those more in harmony with the English Parliament.'

'With Oliver's Parliament, Major. After all he turned out the Members, and admitted his own chosen supporters, and it is these who are making the settlement of Ireland.'

'Indeed. And now this mockery of a Parliament has legalised the transportation of the people of Ulster, Munster and Leinster to Connacht.'

'After that it should be easy enough to drive them into the Atlantic. Is that the idea?'

'I'm afraid, Athy, that you have grasped the principle of the Settlement of Ireland. Coote is directing the plan, and if he is able to fulfil his own and the Government's desire, all the inhabitants of Ireland, whether of English or Irish descent, will be cleared out.'

'It can never be done!' said Athy firmly.

'I hope so. But enough can be done to ruin thousands who have been guilty of nothing but fidelity to their religion, and to an unworthy king.'

'And of possessing fine land?'

'That too. Oliver assured Parliament that the war would pay for itself.'

'So we are to be thrown out when we are drained of all we have?'

'That is the intention. But let us drop the painful subject for the present.' And Charleton turned to kind enquiries about the wounded.

Some had recovered sufficiently to leave and the King of Claddagh was anxious to return home, but it was not considered prudent yet.

It had been hard on him to spend so many weeks indoors and at times he seemed to have become a little dazed through having been so long away from his natural way of life. He often asked why Maeve did not come, and sometimes even wondered where Cahal and Carbra were and why they did not visit him. One day he asked Father Anthony.

'You know,' Father Anthony told him, 'that it is not their fault. Pray for them whenever you thing about them.'

Word had come a few days previously that the ship bound for the West Indies had sunk with all aboard. But it was agreed among all the King's friends that no one should speak about the doomed ship, or mention that the boys had been on it.

ELEVEN

The New Order

As time went by Lynch Fitz-Thomas did more and more favours for his friends, or rather his masters, the Round-heads. Among the captives they brought in from raids around the countryside he was able to identify some secular priests and some Franciscan friars, all of whom had been living disguised among the country people. Men like Mathews, Brock and Camell urged the Government to hang them, but there was a majority in favour of 'mercy', that is, of holding them prisoner until they could be sent off to the plantations.

Aran and Bofin Islands had surrendered having held out for more than a year after the fall of Galway, and more than a hundred priests, seized in different parts of the country, had been sent there to await transportation. Huts were built to accommodate them, and the Council allotted sixpence per day for their maintenance, though Hardiman's *History of Galway* records that only twopence per day was actually received.

It is not clear why they were not transported at once, but undoubtedly the fever of fanaticism had abated somewhat, especially among those officers who wanted to make their homes in Ireland, and they opposed the scheme.

Fitz-Thomas was rewarded, however. For two years after the surrender of Galway the remnants of the Fourteen Families were given the shadow of power in local government through the apppointment of a mayor, two sheriffs, a recorder and other officers. True, the mayor and his colleagues were powerless against the military despotism, and were often imprisoned for attempting to function, but even that shadow of authority was too much for the new rulers.

On 25 October 1654, the Council ordered that the mayor and chief magistrates must be English and Protestant, and that all Catholic officers must be removed. Fitz-Ambrose, the mayor, Blake, the recorder, Lynch and Ffrench Fitz-Peter, the sheriffs, were deposed, and Colonel Stubberd, military governor, was appointed mayor, Clarke the recorder, with Dod and Fitz-Thomas the new sheriffs.

If at this point the traitor could have persuaded Gertrude to become his wife he would have tried to brave the detestation felt for him. But he had now lost every shred of Deane's respect, and in general the *Gaillimhe* refused all contact with this enemy and betrayer of their townsmen.

He felt his isolation the more keenly because he knew that no matter what he did for the Roundheads they would never accept him as his own people would have done if he had been a man of principle. He would have been glad then to be back among the persecuted, but it was too late. Meanwhile the Roundheads were happy to use him, but he knew that despite their smiles they did not trust him in anything.

Along among them Charleton did not even pretend. He

45

had always detested Fitz-Thomas and made no secret of it.

Towards the end of Fitz-Thomas's first year as sheriff Stubberd said casually to Charleton one day, 'Did you tell the Loughrea commissioners that you were not going to claim your allottment of Lord Roche's land?'

'No, sir. Why do you ask?'

Charleton had, indeed, almost decided to forgo his 'right' to these forfeited lands, and would have done so gladly if he could thereby ensure that they would have been restored to their rightful owner. He had been discussing with a friend, whose sense of right and wrong he had come to trust, the question as to whether he would be bound in conscience to surrender his claim only to have it given to another who had no such scruples.

Now, however, the Governor told him that he had received a letter from Sir Charles Coote on the subject. It appeared that Fitz-Thomas had secretly applied to the commissioners for these lands, and that some, Coote's own favourites among them, were supporting his application.

'What can the fellow mean?' demanded Charleton indignantly.

'He appears to have got it into his head that you have abandoned your claim. He also thinks he has a claim on the Government.'

'And does this son of Judas think that simply by turning his coat he is to be put on a level with those who have borne the burden and the heat of the day?'

'You don't usually show such heat yourself, Charleton. But if you do not wish to give up your claim. . .'

'Give up my claim to hand it over to Fitz-Thomas? Not likely!'

'Very good. But Coote must be left in no doubt. I rather think Fitz-Thomas feels very uncomfortable in this town and would be glad of a place to settle, even a thousand miles from Galway. And the men backing his appeal could probably endure his absence quite happily too.'

It was thus that Charleton discovered that there was a conspiracy to get Fitz-Thomas out of town, and most conveniently at the expense of someone the new Corporation did not like. The second part of that plot he determined to foil anyhow. Whatever he might do in different circumstances Charleton would not surrender his claim while there was the slightest danger of Fitz-Thomas, or any other grabber getting the prize.

Fitz-Thomas, though it was not to bring much benefit to him, had brought heavy calamities on the town in which his ancestors had lived honourably. Perhaps the calamities might have come anyhow, but his treachery certainly helped the Roundheads' brutal schemes. If any doubt had remained as to their 'settlement' plans there could have been none after they had dismissed the native Corporation of Galway. It became quite clear to the inhabitants that their new masters intended to clear them out altogether.

Charleton and his 'boatman' talked over the state of affairs. Would this oppression continue? Yes and no, said Charleton. So long as Cromwell lived, it would. He had risen to power by resisting despotism and had turned despot himself. He had trampled underfoot the very principles he had professed when fighting the King. So his rule would finally satisfy only those who had done well out of it, and even those only so long as they needed it to make sure of what they had gained.

'Will the King come by his own again?' asked Father Anthony.

'The monarchy will be restored, and you will have further experience of the Stuarts. But do you suppose the Royalists in England care a straw about what the Irish have suffered? Believe me, there are those around the young Charles who would rather see the Irish estates in the hands of those who cut off the King's head than in the hands of the Irish Catholics who bled for him.

'There will be changes in the Government of England,

47

real changes; and in the Government of Ireland I dare say there will be nominal changes—of men rather than of principles. The men will go, but the spirit will remain. But it won't surprise me if many of those who brought Charles I to the block are not more handsomely rewarded under his successor than many whose fathers lost life and possessions on the Royalist side.'

Their conversation had taken place while they sat on the rich grass at the western edge of Hare Island. In the bright morning sun they had a clear view of the town, of the fortress on Mutton Island, and of the heights of Iar-Connacht beyond. To the south the bare Burren stood out, frowning over the Bay, and to the east the wooded peninsula of Ardfry.

'And it is to there,' said Charleton, pointing to the barren limestone hills, 'that the first batch of the transplanted will be sent to live—or die.'

'The Barony of Burren!' gasped Father Anthony. 'Where they say there is not enough wood to hang a man, water to drown him or earth to bury him!'

'The very place, then, for a people who are to be got rid of!'

'It's too shocking to think of.'

A boat with a white sail shot past the island.

'MacRigh's boat!' said Father Anthony. 'He goes two or three times a week to see Maeve. It's hard, but. . . '

'She would be in danger here. Besides, the Claddagh will be cleared out too. Does the King know anything yet about the boys?'

'He believes they are in prison on Aran. He has improved in his mind since he went back to the fishing, but, as he says himself, he'll never be the same man again. If by any chance he learns the fate of the boys it will kill him. But he won't hear of it from his own people, and he has little or no communication with others.'

'And the daughter?'

'She knows that they were sent to work at Aran and she thinks they are held on Bofin now. She is full of hope that good news will come.'

TWELVE

'Root them out'

'Now I could dance with joy and thanksgiving as did King David before the Lord!' cried Sheriff Mathews.

His outburst of pious jubilation arose out of the order of 30 October 1655, made by the Lord-Deputy and Council to clear out all the old inhabitants of Galway and replace them with an English colony. The order was to be enforced by Sir Charles Coote, Lord President of Connacht, a man well fitted to do the work of Attila, and possessed of willing helpers in the sheriffs just appointed, Mathews and Camell.

When this news reached the Governor he sent for Deane and they were closeted for several hours. There was plenty of good wine, of which Stubberd drank freely and Deane sparingly.

The question was, what was Deane to do? The Governor thought he could save him by assigning his premises and stock to himself, but what about Gertrude? There was a special difficulty here because Fitz-Thomas had lodged a complaint that Charleton and Miss Deane were engaged to be married.

Deane denied this. It was, as he pointed out, legally impossible in any case, but even if it were not, he would oppose it as something foreign to the traditions and principles of his family. Stubberd told him that he was expecting a visit from Coote the following day, and that it was likely that this alleged violation of Ireton's Ordinance would be discussed.

However, the Governor was not particularly interested in the subject. He was preoccupied with the projected new settlement of Galway, and was unusually cheerful, talking with a freedom which surprised even Deane who knew him fairly well. Coote was coming, he said, and Coote was a great fellow, but he knew something more than Coote and if it went to a trial of strength, then Oliver would have to stand by him, Peter Stubberd.

'The hand that did what this hand has done can do something still. I tell you, Stephen, *this hand knows the strength of Charles Stuart's neck!*'

He jumped up and went to the door to make sure no one was there. He did not hear the light footsteps that hurried away, and he saw no one.

'We have been good friends, Stephen,' he said, sitting down again. 'Let us continue to be so. I am blamed for consorting with sinners because of you, but I can leave such cant to crawling things like Mathews and Camell.

'Oliver knows how to turn religion to account and to overlook it when it suits him. When he was in Dublin he more than once dined with someone he knew to be a Jesuit. And Coote, who is now all fury against papists, was at one time glad to negotiate with them.

'Put your trust in me, Stephen, and I will stand between you and Coote.'

Stubberd's friendship with Deane, like his cruelty to others, was due to his avarice. He could have imprisoned Deane, or banished him; he could have put him to death by torture without feeling any remorse. But he had enough sense not to kill the goose that laid the golden egg.

Coote was a more ferocious type. His grand ideal was the extermination of the Irish race. Until this was done there would be no security.

'What we must do,' he said in the Governor's apartment the following morning, 'is to take precautions that we do not lose what we have gained by so much blood and sacrifice, and we have no security while the old occupiers are permitted to remain. For the present we will have to let them settle on this side of the Shannon, but for that very reason we must make the towns, Galway and Sligo especially, strong garrisons. We cannot look on our work as perfect while any of the old stock remains.'

'Yet you are sending more of them to Clare and Connacht.'

'For the present that is unavoidable. We have to clear them out of three provinces. We cannot ship them all away at once, and we cannot hang or shoot so many because of our reputation abroad. Better send them into the more desolate parts of Connacht and Clare and let them contend with Nature and one another. Later we can send them to the plantations.'

'Admirable!' cried Stubberd. 'It's the Lord Protector all over!'

'The Lord Protector!' exclaimed Coote. 'He is one of the many difficulties in our way. He reads petitions from persons liable to transportation and sends us recommendations in their favour. Lord Ikerrin, a Popish recusant, had the audacity to go to Whitehall in person and the Lord Protector wrote recommending some provision for him. Oliver in favour of a papist rebel! But we have made up our minds to listen to no such prayers, even from Oliver. And yet, would you believe it, in many cases our own officers take sides with the rebels against the commissioners.'

Stubberd then mentioned the matter of Fitz-Thomas's report about Miss Deane.

'There we have a new crop of troubles,' complained Coote. 'Ireton's Ordinance is a dead letter already. Our fellows cannot hold out against the charms of the 'women of Canaan' as Mathews would say. Though I don't think I would trust that same Jack Mathews very far. Is there anything in this allegation?'

'I have questioned both Charleton and the girl's father,'

said Stubberd. 'Both deny it. I fancy the chief ground for the allegation is that Fitz-Thomas has been an unsuccessful suitor, and believes that Charleton is the obstacle.'

'Then let the matter drop. We have more urgent work to do than enquiring into imaginary love matches.'

The enquiry would, in any case, have produced nothing.

Very early that morning, hidden by a drizzling fog, Gertrude had been rowed across to her uncle's home, Tyrone House. She had had a timely warning that if Fitz-Thomas and Mathews had their way she might be brought before a military court, for the newly-appointed Sheriff Mathews might have overruled Stubberd. Happily Coote had now dismissed the whole business but it was still better for Gertrude to be out of the town before the dread decision of the Council to clear out the inhabitants could be put into force.

Maeve was still at Tyrone House, and the King of Claddagh was happy that she should be so far out of reach of the *Bodach Sasanach*. Gertrude, too, was glad to have an opportunity to cultivate closer relations with her uncle, Mr Ffrench, who in common with others disliked what they saw as too close a connection between Mr Deane and the Governor.

The brutal order of 30 October 1655 was carried out by Coote with unrelenting severity. The inhabitants were driven out of the town in mid-winter and forced to take shelter in ditches and cabins without fire or sufficient clothing, while Coote received the thanks of the Lord-Deputy and his Council for his efficiency.

But the attempts to establish a new English colony in Galway failed. Negotiations which had begun with the city of Gloucester, offering property and a new way of life to any of its citizens who cared to come to Galway, ended in failure. And that in spite of the fact that they were given the added inducement that 'noe Irish are permitted to inhabit in the cittie, or within three miles thereof.'

While the 'godly' were at first delighted to have none of the 'unclean nation' among them, they soon found it inconvenient. Who would do the menial jobs when everyone thought himself entitled to better things? So, those who were able and willing to work gradually came back into the town. The three mile limit vanished too when it became plain that nothing was gained but much lost by having this territory empty and unproductive. Better to have the country folk bringing in their produce than to have those inside the walls dependent on forays into the desolate surrounding area.

Thus common sense eventually defeated fanaticism but even in the short time it took much misery and irreparable wrong were inflicted. And the people who had had little to lose came back more easily than those who had been deprived of valuable properties.

THIRTEEN

Esker-in-the-Bog

Gertrude was beginning to feel quite at home in her place of refuge. Some refugees from Galway had found some shelter in the neighbourhood, and she had occupied herself with a round of daily visits among them, doing what she could to console and help the victims of the frenzied tyranny.

Maeve MacRigh often accompanied her in this charitable work, but after a time she was called away to the very grave dangers of the Claddagh to nurse her father, who for the first time in his life was seriously ill.

However, a few days after Maeve left, horsemen were

seen passing and repassing in the vicinity of Tyrone House, and while they did not interfere with anyone Gertrude and her friends were disturbed. Fearing that if Fitz-Thomas discovered her whereabouts he would not scruple to take her away by force Father Anthony then suggested an idea which she accepted.

So at an early hour on the following morning a heavy lumbering carriage drove along a zigzag causeway or *tochar* which appeared to lead into a kind of swamp broken here and there by hillocks and ridges covered with furze and hazel, and patches of short grass. From these ridges or *eiscirs* of limestone the locality takes its name, Esker. At certain points the *tochar* was scarcely above the level of the surrounding bog, and at times the water would actually cover portions of it.

The vehicle drew up at a cluster of cabins in front of which stood a pleasant-faced youth who smiled a welcome as Father Anthony stepped out of it, followed by Gertrude and her uncle, Mr Ffrench. Father Anthony introduced them to the young man who was, in fact, Donough, the youngest son of the King of Claddagh, the boy who was preparing for the religious life.

The little cluster of cabins nestled under the shoulder of a great ridge and was partly enclosed by a wall so that little more than the thatch could be seen from the *tochar*. The inhabitants were none other than the Dominicans who had been expelled from the Dominican Abbey of Athenry. Through the kindness of friends they had been provided with shelter in this place which was sufficiently bleak and inaccessible as not to arouse the greed even of the Cromwellians.

The visitors went first into the church, a rude timber shanty which looked like a cowshed. There were no seats and only the altar suggested its purpose. They attended the community Mass and then Father Anthony brought his party into the refectory, a cabin in which ten or twelve people sat on forms on each side of a deal table. In spite of the drastic change in their conditions the friars were remarkably cheerful. Only the elderly prior, who suffered greatly from the damp and discomfort, seemed a little downcast. However, Mr Ffrench, while he expressed his sympathy, tried to cheer him up by reminding him that most great monasteries had been established in desolate places, and been turned into places of great beauty through the labours of their inhabitants.

'Who knows,' he said, 'but that this Esker-in-the-Bog may become a thing of glory to the Dominican Order?'

It was a fine morning and Father Anthony took his friends for a walk along the top of the ridge from where they saw a second parallel ridge to the south of them, and men planting the slopes to make a garden around the new settlement.

'Now,' said Father Anthony, after they had walked some way along the crest of the ridge, 'you will have a better view of the neighbourhood.'

Gertrude was surprised at the wide range of the view before her, and the place seemed much more interesting than she had imagined when they were driving along the *tochar* earlier on.

'What a lot of old castles!' she exclaimed, pointing to five or six to be seen to the south along the course of the Kiltulla River, and to others looming further away in the distance.

'Yes, indeed,' replied Father Anthony. 'Those and many others around County Galway are a witness to the power and influence of the De Burgos, and to the long struggle between them and the older inhabitants. That,' he said, pointing north-west, 'is Bermingham Castle. It is called after the man who conquered the O'Connors, and a little later overcame their Scottish ally, Edward Bruce. To the left of it is our old Abbey of St Dominic. The poor prior often comes up here to have a look at the place from which he was driven out, even though it upsets him deeply, especially when he hears the drums and bugles of the soldiers.'

Then turning away from the view of old Athenry he pointed out a castle to the north-east which belonged to the O'Dalys who were well-known to the Fourteen Families; and also Kiltulla Castle, the home of the D'Arcys, great lawyers and fearless patriots. South again he showed her Dunsandle which was then in the hands of the Clanrickarde family. 'This old neighbourhood,' he observed, 'though it looks waste and dreary now, has had a stirring history.'

Gertrude was not to remain at Esker. The plan was for her to go on to Laragh, one of the old castles along the Kiltulla River. It was occupied by a member of the O'Daly family whose wife Delia had been at school with her in the Dominican Convent in Galway, and was in fact a relative. Gertrude had promised to visit Laragh Castle after Delia married, but owing to the war she had not been able to do so.

Father Anthony had earlier sent a messenger to tell Mr and Mrs O'Daly that Gertrude would be coming; and the messenger returned before the little party had come back from their walk on the ridge to say that the O'Dalys were going to Athenry on business and would call and bring Gertrude home with them on their way back.

As Father Anthony and his friends returned from their survey of the neighbourhood a handbell was rung from the door of the little church and all joined the friars in saying the *Angelus.*

FOURTEEN

'One of the transplanted'

Darkness had settled on the dreary bog-flats of Esker. The evening was calm and the silence profound except for the cries of the water-fowl, the only songbirds, as Father Anthony said, which had yet discovered the way to that dismal swamp.

An hour or so after nightfall a cry for help startled the inmates of the new Priory. Someone had got stuck in the bog. It might be the O'Dalys. It might be friend or foe; but either way the friars would answer the cry. A Dominican brother and two men who lived on the premises went out with a lantern and brought back a man who had missed the *tochar* and got so deep into the muddy water that he was afraid to move for fear of drowning.

They brought him into the kitchen to wash and suggested that he change his wet clothes, but the few spare items he had with him were also soaked.

'With your permission,' he said, 'I'll dry out at the peat fire. I'm well used to a wetting, but not to such a means of drying.'

As he stood before the fire it was evident that he was no ordinary tramp, though his attire was shabby enough. There was something in his bearing, Father Anthony thought, which poverty did not disguise and calamity could not obliterate.

'I'll explain how I got here,' the stranger said, 'by stating what I really am—*one of the transplanted.*'

After evening prayers he was brought to the prior's room where he told his harrowing tale; a tale in which Gertrude and her uncle took an intense interest.

Maurice, Viscount Roche, late of Castletownroche in County Cork, had had many trials.

In the campaign of 1650 his chief castle was besieged by a detachment of Oliver's army. Lady Roche was in command of the castle and for four days she offered a spirited resistance and would have held out for longer but for heavy fire from a battery erected on the other side of the Awbeg. Two years later the new masters of Munster revenged themselves for her defiance by hanging her on a charge of murder, though there was evidence that she was twenty miles away at the time and knew nothing of the crime.

In 1654 Lord Roche was dispossessed of all his property, and his estates were given to Colonel Widenham who had betrayed Youghal to the Cromwellians. Roche and his four young daughters were turned out with no means of support except the charity of others, and one of the girls died from exposure and hunger.

For ten months he had kept applying to the authorities in Dublin for help, but all he got was an order to the Loughrea Commissioners to give him some land provisionally. He had set out on foot for Connacht and another six months went by before he was assigned land in the Nephin Beg area. The land was waste and unprofitable but even at that it had been assigned to others before he could take possession of it.

Now he was as far from having a settlement as when he started.

The story was especially distressing to Gertrude, for it was a portion of Lord Roche's confiscated lands which had been allotted to Charleton.

'I have talked long about myself,' said Lord Roche, 'as if I were the only victim. Jordan Roche of Limerick had a huge estate; now his daughters support themselves by taking in washing.'

And yet, thought Gertrude, they were happier than would be the wife of a man who had taken the home and lands of people hunted out without means or prospects.

Lord Roche gave the company a moving account of the sufferings of the transplanted. Though they forfeited house and lands they were supposed to have the right to their movables. But how could these be taken from the east or the south over to the west, and in the depth of winter? Besides, there was little welcome for them in the west, and no wonder. Confusion and bribery reigned among the Loughrea Commissioners. If a man succeeded in obtaining a bit of bog or a bleak mountainside he might find it already settled; or another and stronger applicant might come and drive him and his family off again.

The prior, who had listened compassionately to Lord Roche, then spoke. 'Do not imagine, my lord,' he said, 'that I am not sympathetic, but does it not seem that some sort of retribution has come upon the Anglo-Irish gentry?'

'No, Father Prior, I don't understand it so.'

'Was there ever greater cruelty and vandalism than that which accompanied the Desmond wars of eighty years ago?'

'But Desmond and his friends were rebels!'

'Just what the Roundheads say of you and your friends.'

Father Anthony and Mr Ffrench intervened to turn the conversation, but Father Dominic had a will of his own and was not to be diverted.

'Who are the people,' he continued, 'who have suffered most in the present transplantation? Are they not the descendants of the very men who since the Plantagenets have tried to root out the native Irish? And now they have been treated as mere Irish themselves.'

'We are all Irish now, Father Dominic,' interposed Mr Ffrench.

'Ay, Cromwell and his following will tell you so! But it is not so long, only 1518, since the Galway burghers ordered that "neither O ne Mac shall strutte ne swaggere thro the streets of Galway".

'We may say,' went on the prior, warming to his subject, 'that because the Catholic Lords of the Pale *would be*

59

English and not Irish we are in our present unhappy position. If you had made common cause with the Irish when the troubles began in '41, or even later; if you had been able to put aside racial jealousy and appointed the hero of Benburb as commander-in-chief, the regicides would not be where they are today.'

'Preston was a brave man,' put in Father Anthony.

'He had courage and ability,' agreed Father Dominic, 'but jealousy of the mere Irish paralysed him. Yes, my lord, your pitiful jealousy of the old stock was your ruin and ours too. You allowed the King's cause to fall into the hands of Ormonde, who betrayed Dublin and whose mismanagement opened the door to Cromwell, the man who really hated the Irish and their religion. If you could have supported the one man capable of defeating Cromwell, Owen Roe O'Neill, your story, and mine, would have been very different. For no other reason than that he was Irish he was thrust aside. Now, you may chew on that, my lord.'

'I have many bitter things to chew on, Father, and often I have little else to chew on.'

'Well, we must make the best of matters as they stand,' rejoined the prior, and he signalled to one of the community to bring in something to cheer the company.

An earthenware jar and some wooden drinking vessels were brought and the prior, turning to Lord Roche said, with a very different expression, 'I find, my lord, that in this damp and gloomy situation a little *uisge beatha,* used in moderation, has great sustaining power.'

The *uisge beatha* had indeed a magical effect on all present. The gloom which had hung over them was put aside and for an hour or so the victims of oppression wrested a little happiness out of the tyrant's grasp.

The arrival of the O'Dalys brought an exchange of warm greetings all round, and as Mr O'Daly took his cup of *uisge beatha* and stood in front of the blazing peat fire he told the company of the adventure which had befallen his wife and himself on their journey.

'You did not meet the Roundheads, I trust?' asked Father Anthony.

'We did indeed,' he replied. 'We had some business in Athenry and were about to start on our way here when a buff-coat officer came to tell us we were wanted at Bermingham Castle. When we arrived we were put into a room and kept there until about two hours ago when we were brought before the commander of the garrison, who was with an officer from Galway, a Major Charleton I believe.'

Gertrude started slightly, and Mr O'Daly continued.

'And what do you suppose was our offence? My wife Delia had tied a ribbon in such a way that the Roundhead officer thought it was a cross flaunted in his face. The commander seemed irritated by his zeal, and ordered us to be freed immediately, and Major Charleton apologised to us. But we were lucky in these times to get away.'

The reason why Charleton happened to be at Bermingham Castle was that he was on his way to Loughrea to see Coote about his allotted land. He was by now entitled to leave the army but he had remained on at Stubberd's request as his aide-de-camp, for the Governor valued him more highly than the canting zealots around him. But Charleton was growing weary of the job, and he was concerned that certain people were trying to deprive him of his land.

Coote listened; but he told Charleton to return to Galway until further notice. However his journey had not been entirely wasted for Charleton met with Lord Roche who was making a last attempt to procure somewhere to settle.

Charleton, moved by the sight of such destitution, told Lord Rocne that he would happily forgo his claim if the lands were returned to their rightful owner.

'My good sir,' said the nobleman, 'it would be folly. You would lose, and I should gain nothing. I am pleased to find that some of my property is going to a man of integrity. Even in my own interest I would urge you to hold on, for

I would wish to lay my bones among my kinfolk, and for that last privilege I must be indebted to the occupier who would allow me a few feet of my once vast estates.'

Charleton had already been advised to take his portion, and he was now determined to assert his claim against all comers.

But what would Gertrude say?

FIFTEEN
Around Laragh

Laragh Castle had been built to command a ford on the Kiltulla River by which, in fact, it was surrounded except for a causeway on the west. From the warder's tower the view extended up and down the river as it meandered through pleasant green meadows which contrasted cheerfully with the stretches of bog beyond them on the one side and the boulder-strewn plateau on the other.

It was no longer garrisoned for all arms had been surrendered, and the few landowners who had not yet been disturbed knew that they remained on sufferance and that their best defence lay in submission to the Commonwealth Parliament.

When the weather was fine Gertrude and Delia O'Daly would go up to the warder's tower and spend hours talking over old schooldays and school friends, and about the tragic events which had brought so many once affluent families to destitution. Between them they could reckon a pretty strong muster of kinfolk who had succumbed to suffering and sorrow.

'We have been fortunate,' Gertrude would say.

'We have indeed. Surely, the worst is over now, but still we can't be sure. In any case, things will never be the same again.'

'Oh never! It is almost a reproach to have a home and enough to live on when so many have neither.'

'Well, at any rate, we certainly have an obligation to help less fortunate people.'

Occasionally Delia would refer to Charleton, but Gertrude never mentioned his name unless it was unavoidable.

'Why do people persist in speaking to me about him?' she asked one day. 'He has never given any cause for it, and I am sure I haven't.'

'Well, I feel certain that you could not think of marrying a Puritan, and settling down on a confiscated estate.'

'Does anyone think I could?'

'No, of course not. But leave aside his Puritanism, and the fact that he would be taking allotted lands. How would you consider his personal merits?'

'I should find no fault with him under those conditions. Now, may we drop the subject? Some fine day we must take a walk to the top of those hills.'

The hills lay to the north and west of Laragh, and were connected with the *eiscirs* already described. They consisted of the same limestone but were much larger and higher so that from a distance they seemed like a miniature mountain chain standing out above the bog-flats.

The weather remained bad, and the girls were occupied in visiting sick and poor people in the bogside cabins, so that it was towards the end of May before they found an opportunity to climb the mimic mountain range. The hillocks were covered with clumps of furze or hazel or bracken, and there was a close crop of new grass due to the limestone and the spring rain. Multitudes of rabbits scampered out of their way as they walked, and they saw a flock of sheep almost as timid and wild as the rabbits.

When they reached the top of the highest hill in the group they looked southward into a number of grassy hollows and cup-shaped depressions. Over on the margin of the bog they saw groups of men and women cutting turf.

The men cut the brick-shaped pieces with a slane and the girls carried it to the 'spreading-ground' to dry out. The men's white jackets of home-made flannel and the red handkerchiefs which the girls wore on their heads made a colourful scene, and there was plenty of joking and singing going on as they worked.

'What happy people!' exclaimed Gertrude.

'Do you envy them?' Delia asked her.

'Well, I could almost wish to fling off my shoes, tie a red handkerchief on my head and join them. One would think there was no cause for sorrow among them.'

It is that buoyancy of spirit which has kept the Irish race in being,' said Delia. 'Now, let's have a look at the western side.'

Below on this side was a lake and in the centre of it rose a great mound of the same stone formation with hazel, blackthorn and furze growing all over it.

'I'd love to go over to that little island,' said Gertrude. 'Look, there's a boat!'

In a small boat on the lake two men were casting lines.

'Let's try to get down to the water,' said Delia. 'They're coming across towards us'

As the two girls scrambled down through the scrub and furze they saw that the occupants of the boat were Father Anthony and Donough MacRigh. They agreed to the girls' request to be rowed over to the island, but when they reached it young Donough stayed in the boat and, had they noticed as they clambered ashore, they would have seen that he appeared to be rather uneasy.

They wandered around exploring the little island and came upon one of the cup-shaped depressions they had noticed from the hill, except that this one was partly concealed by brush which grew all around it.

Gertrude took a few steps into it but suddenly retreated looking startled. Father Anthony went on and to his astonishment came on two young men hiding there.

'Carbra Conneely and Conor MacRigh!' he exclaimed.

Gertrude's alarm gave way to agreeable surprise. Surely these were the two young men she had heard had gone down with the West Indian ship, and Carbra was the one to have married the King of Claddagh's daughter when they were separated through the cruel raids carried out on the orders of Colonel Stubberd.

'How and when did you get here?' Father Anthony asked anxiously, for clearly they must have had help to get to the island.

They told him that they had been rowed there that very morning by Donough which explained why the boy had seemed ill at ease when the three went ashore. Carbra explained that they had managed to escape from captivity the day before the doomed ship had sailed for the West Indies, and had been through many desperate adventures since which would take a long time to relate. They had thought of Esker as a place where they might find shelter for a time and get news of their families and friends.

Father Anthony invited them to come across to the priory for food but Carbra replied that Donough had brought them enough for the moment and that what they needed more than anything else—for they had had none for nearly a week—was rest without fear of being discovered by the Roundheads. After that they would do whatever Father Anthony advised.

So it was agreed; and the fugitives were fast asleep before the little party had left the island.

Meanwhile the news from Galway was not entirely bad. Father Anthony had been 'across the water' several times in the past month. The worst thing was that the King of Claddagh was keeping to his bed. He did not seem to be sick, but he had lost all interest in what was going on around him. He was in a cabin about three miles west of Galway, but many of his friends had already returned to the Claddagh after the 'clearance'. His Council wanted to bring him back and had re-erected a cabin for him on the site of the one destroyed, for they believed that it would rouse him to be in his old surroundings again.

Since the hoped-for English colony would not come to Galway the Roundheads were finding it useful to allow the old inhabitants back to do necessary work and to occupy the empty houses which were falling into ruin.

Not all the inhabitants were fanatics, and fanaticism in any case was declining. The more thoughtful knew that back in England Oliver had become unpopular by going too far and that no successor would dare to imitate him.

Big changes were coming, and the more worldly-wise were planning to make friends with the 'Mammon of Iniquity', that is, with the very people they had previously condemned and persecuted.

SIXTEEN

Carbra's Story

Before nightfall Carbra Conneely and Cahal MacRigh were persuaded to leave their island refuge for the priory where they were brought to Father Anthony's room and there Carbra gave an account of all that had befallen them since they were removed from the fort on Mutton Island.

'When we were taken to the Connemara coast,' he said, 'we were put to work on the huts and fortifications for the siege of Aran. Later we had to teach the soldiers how to catch fish. Cahal would be taken out in one boat and myself in another. There were always two soldiers armed with swords in each boat, and we were never allowed to go far out. Meanwhile we had discovered that we were to be sent to the West Indies, and we began to think about how we might escape.

'At last one day we were put into the same boat, though still with two soldiers. A breeze sprang up and we were ordered to make for the shore. We ran the boat into shallow water and shot pretty close to a large rock. Both soldiers turned round startled, and we raised our oars and knocked them into the water. Before they could recover their balance we pulled away with all our might and were soon out of their sight.

'We pulled towards Spiddal and got into a rocky cave about three miles west of the village. We let the boat go because it might identify us, and we hid in the scrub for five days, collecting shell-fish for food. After that we ventured inland and got a change of clothes.'

Even in the wild and desolate district towards Ballina-hinch, the boys reported the 'settlement' was going on. Lots of the transplanted Ulster people had settled in Leitrim, Sligo and the north-east of Mayo; but they were moved on again to the bleakest parts of Mayo and Iàr-Connacht. Some of these had only just arrived and they had no kind of shelter. Women, children and old men had died on the way, and some died after they arrived, as if they could no longer face the struggle to live in such conditions.

'Cahal and I stayed for a while among them,' Carbra continued, 'and helped to put up shanties for people and cattle. But although we knew it was dangerous we found ourselves gradually moving nearer to Corrib, for we wanted to know how things were at home. One evening near Barna we were almost caught by a mounted patrol. We made for the beach and found a currach and rowed away. At daybreak we were near Black Head over on the Clare side so we hauled up the currach and hid it where we could find it again if we needed to. I hope we'll be able to repay the owner some day.'

Among the Burren hills the fugitives found even greater misery than on the other side of the Bay. The sufferings of the Claddagh people during their temporary exile were as nothing compared with those of the people of Kilkenny, Westmeath, Longford, Tipperary and elsewhere who had been transplanted to Burren and Corcomroe. Every kind of habitation had been burned down and the famine was so acute at one time that people had been forced to kill their cart-horses and eat them. There were even gruesome stories of people reduced to eating the remains of those who had died of starvation.

'All the time,' Carbra went on, 'there was a longing on us to return to the old place. We were on our way to Bally-vaughan when we saw a cruiser in the bay, so we took off to the hills again towards Kinvarra.'

Once again they missed capture by a hair's breadth from a cavalry raiding party among whom Carbra saw Lynch Fitz-Thomas. The raiders retreated when a volley of mus-ketry assailed them from a band of so-called 'Tories' hidden in brambles and boulders. The 'Tories' who were on their way to Portumna forced Cahal and Carbra to come with them, although they knew nothing about firearms. How-ever, the boys managed to separate from them during the night and once again hid until hunger forced them to move. They decided then to make for the Dominican refuge in Esker bogs, for they knew that there they would not die of starvation.

They were very anxious now to get home on account of the King and Maeve, but Father Anthony urged them to stay for a few days until he came back from a visit to Corrib and would have more news about what was happening there.

The two young men stayed inside the priory enclosure for the week—although they were not used to the quiet, regular life—and helped to build a dry-stone wall to enclose some pigs which had lately been added to the priory's live-stock.

Father Anthony's first news on his return was that the King was back in the Claddagh.

'We had him taken there,' he told them, 'wrapped in a

blanket in his own white-sailed hooker from Gentian Hill to the Corrib side. Then we carried him into the new cabin. But the best news is that Colonel Stubberd has been persuaded to give orders that he is not to be disturbed. Even Stubberd can be generous, but the chief credit belongs to Major Charleton and Mr **Deane**.'

Father Anthony did not say that while Maeve was overjoyed the news of their safety seemed to make little impression on the King who was still sunk in a kind of torpor and did not believe it. The only thing which would rouse him would be for him to see the boys for himself, but Father Anthony was not sure that it would be safe yet.

Carbra, however, suggested that they ought to go over. It could be dangerous he knew but they would be willing to take the risk. Father Anthony advised against it for the moment. There had been a number of raids recently, he said, on the 'property' of the new occupiers of Galway by dispossessed men who called themselves 'Tories', and because of this both the day and night patrols had been increased. It would be especially dangerous for the two of them since they were escaped prisoners.

Father Anthony then journeyed on to Laragh Castle with a message for Gertrude from her father, and was greatly disturbed when he came back to find that during his absence Carbra and Cahal had set out for the Claddagh. They had told Donough that they would only be gone a few hours; they knew a way to get in and out, they said, without meeting the buff-coats.

They had left immediately after Father Anthony set out for Laragh, so they now had had about three hours' start. It would be hard to overtake them but Father Anthony decided to go after them all the same, for he might still be able to come between them and danger.

'If they fall into the hands of the Roundheads,' he observed, 'it will be a full stop to Carbra's story.'

SEVENTEEN
Misadventure

A dark, gloomy night had settled down upon the water, its murkiness increased by a fine drizzle, when the boat pulled by the two young men drew close by Mutton Island.

'If we can get past the island without being seen. . .' said Carbra, 'we'll be all right.'

But they did not get past unseen—or at least unheard. The sound of their oars was heard by the sentry on the castle walls and as the boatman did not heed his challenge he fired a musket shot in their direction, and almost immediately a boat manned by four soldiers streaked out in pursuit.

As they were in danger of being caught before reaching the river mouth the boys kept south of the island as if running for Barna. The pursuers were four to two and could have overtaken them in open water, but the inshore race hampered them.

When they were opposite Mount Gentian the fugitives brought their boat safely through a maze of huge boulders blocking the entrance to the creek. The pursuing boat followed but stuck on some of the smaller submerged stones.

'We'll have time to carry the boat over the ridge,' said Cahal, 'and run back before they can get off.'

On the other side of the ridge they slid the boat into the water and resumed their flight, but to their dismay they found that the Roundheads were still after them, though not so close. This time the pursuers were on their guard against being drawn in too close, but they were aiming at keeping between the two young men and Mutton Island.

Carbra and Cahal knew the rugged coast so well that

they could run alarmingly near to the rocks without endangering their boat, and driving in towards the boulders they allowed the Roundheads to pass while they turned in around the headland where Salthill now stands. Shortly before midnight they turned into Lower Salthill Bay and rowed on to a point where the creek curved round a kind of crag covered with stunted blackthorn.

'We can leave the boat here,' said Carbra, 'and walk round the hill.'

They dragged the boat from the water intending to hide it in the brushwood.

'Halt!' shouted a hoarse voice, and the two young men found themselves in the hands of five soldiers who were patrolling the area, probably because it was near the track leading to Barna and Spiddal.

'Who are you and what are you doing in this place?' demanded the leader.

The astonished captives who only partly understood the questions could not reply in English.

'Shackle them!' came the order. 'Take them to the citadel.'

The unfortunate fugitives were all but crushed by this heart-freezing disappointment. After so many toils and perils, and just as they had almost reached home, to have fallen into the hands of the dreaded enemmy with now only the prospect of an early and violent death before them was almost too much. They broke down and wept bitterly as they were dragged past the end of the Claddagh and through the three great gates guarding the West Bridge.

They were thrown into a small, vaulted room in the citadel, and when the light of the warder's lantern vanished as he slammed the iron door a blackness of spirit descended upon them matching the gloom and damp of the cell.

'If we had only listened to Father Anthony's advice,' groaned Cahal in near despair.

'What advice would he give us now?' asked Carbra.

'Why, he would tell us that the hand of the Lord is more powerful than the hand of the *Sasanach*, and that we must ask his help.'

'Then let's do that,' said Carbra, and wet and cold though they were they knelt down on the flags and said a prayer. Then famished and exhausted they fell asleep on the stone floor. Yet, wretched though their lot was at that moment, they were not the least happy people in Galway.

Late the following morning, having been given some bread and water, they were led out and paraded in the courtyard before a group of officers.

'A rich capture!' remarked Lynch Fitz-Thomas to the captain of the citadel.

'Why?'

'Tories!'

'Tories?' asked Mathews. He seldom condescended to speak to Fitz-Thomas but his curiosity was aroused.

'These men were in the band of Tories in the mountains above Gort who recently fired on our patrol,' replied Fitz-Thomas.

'I thought you reported that they were so well hidden that you could not see them,' interposed Lieutenant-Colonel Humphrey Hurd.

'I saw those two at the outpost,' claimed Fitz-Thomas, 'and it was they who gave the order to fire.'

'The Lord has delivered them into our hands,' exulted Mathews. 'We'll hang them on the Great Gate Tower.'

'Perhaps,' observed Charleton drily, 'you might be good enough to allow the Governor to have a word in the matter before you proceed to hanging.'

Mathews, turning aside to his friends Camell and Brock, whispered that Charleton was a Tory at heart, but aloud he said, 'the people who screen such men are as bad as they are.'

His intention was to stir up feeling against Charleton, but the majority were on the Major's side and believed that no action should be taken until the Governor returned from his visit to Coote in Loughrea.

The prisoners consequently were returned to their dark cell, and on Charleton's intervention the captain of the citadel ordered the removal of their shackles.

Father Anthony had lost no time in setting out after the young men hoping to overtake them and persuade them against their foolhardy expedition. He went first to Tyrone House and finding no trace of them was about to be rowed out to a herring boat when word was brought to him that a man about three miles away was dying and wanted a priest. While Father Anthony was attending to the sick call Carbra and Cahal walked straight into the hands of the enemy.

The following morning, in his role as Charleton's boatman, Father Anthony was waiting at Wood Quay when the Major joined him after the confrontation at the citadel at which he had saved the boys from being summarily hanged.

Nothing would be done until the Governor returned, Charleton told him, though if Mathews and his party had had their way the prisoners would now be dangling under the clock over the East Gate.

'But I am afraid the case is serious for the poor fellows,' he continued.

'It is certain that they are innocent,' said Father Anthony.

'I have no doubt of it. But innocence is no proof against perjury. The statement of Fitz-Thomas is positive and precise. Who is to contradict him?'

'Would evidence as to character be received?'

'Yes. But how could it be given without going into past events? So far no one seems to connect them with the escape in Connemara, but if you mention their previous history how can you guard against bringing all that out? It's the old story of rushing against the rocks in order to escape the whirlpool.

'There will be loud calls for their blood,' continued Charleton, 'and the Governor's sense of right and wrong is

73

not to be relied upon. But he hates Mathews and when he hears, as he shall hear for I will see to that, that Mathews was for hanging them without an hour's delay, he may be more merciful. A lot will depend on his mood when he comes to hear the case.

Did the Claddagh know of their capture, he asked Father Anthony, who replied that he believed that so far no one on that side of the river knew anything. When their boat was found people would ask questions, but he thought all bad news should be kept out of the King's cabin for as long as possible.

Charleton stepped ashore at Tirrelan Castle. He was in direct command of the garrison there, and since the midnight forays by Tories in the neighbouring areas he was obliged to visit it nearly every day.

As he would be engaged for some time the 'boatman' pulled across to the west side and rested in quiet water between two small banks. Presently a brown-sailed hooker laden with fuel came down midstream. Father Anthony recognised someone aboard it and soon the little boat was alongside the larger craft and drifting downstream with it.

After a short conversation with a man wearing a slouched, glazed hat who leaned over the hooker's side Father Anthony pulled back towards the west side and up to his previous mooring between the two banks. His little circular tour could easily have been watched from the castle battlements, but there was nothing remarkable in it. Boats were constantly coming and going and hailing one another. The sentry on the battlements could not have heard what was said, and had no reason to attach any importance to the episode.

EIGHTEEN

Patients and Patience

Stubberd was very angry on his return to hear that Mathews had proposed the execution of the prisoners, though his concern was not for them but for himself. He had long suspected that Mathews was trying to oust him from the governorship, and while he was in Loughrea he had discovered that the Mathews clique had indeed secretly approached the Lord-Deputy about the matter. There was no reason to suppose that they would succeed, but the whole business had put Stubberd into a very bad mood. He would have released the prisoners then and there just to show Mathews who was Governor but Dod and Fitz-Thomas hinted to him that this would probably bring a censure from Parliament. So he fixed a time to hear their case, though his humour boded them no good. However, there was clearly a great change in the times when a trial of any kind was being considered.

Stubberd was engaged on other matters for two days, but on the third, as he had to inspect the citadel anyway, he said he would see the alleged Tories and listen to the case.

On that morning he was standing on the stone steps leading to his apartments when a seafaring man wearing an oilskin and a slouched, glazed hat and carrying a basket of shell-fish spoke to him.

'Want any Burren oysters, your honour? Look at them lobsters,' and then suddenly, 'Help his honour! He's going to faint.'

Indeed the Governor would have fallen down the steps if Charleton and Hurd who were near him had not supported him. A crowd gathered and in the excitement the oysterman disappeared leaving his basket behind him. The Governor was carried to bed and a search made for the seafaring man, but no one could remember seeing him.

Dr Athy was summoned at once. He and Mr Deane had been the first of the original residents to be allowed back into Galway after the town had been cleared by Coote. They had been recalled, in fact, by Stubberd himself who found it in his own interest to have them nearby.

'It's the old complaint,' the doctor whispered to Charleton having examined the Governor.

'As serious as before?'

'I'm afraid so, and we no longer have the nurses who brought him round then.'

'There is one who might help,' suggested Charleton hesitantly.

'Gertrude?'

'Yes. But I suppose it's out of the question?'

'I don't know,' returned Dr Athy. 'Her father has already asked her to come back but she is not much inclined to. She doesn't like her father's association with your people. But I think she might come if we appealed to her charity. Besides, it would be better to have Stubberd for Governor than that odious Mathews.'

'She seems very much at home at Laragh,' remarked Charleton casually.

'Well, Delia is like a sister. They were brought up together in the Dominican convent, and of course she feels safer there. However, if she ran into any unpleasantness here she could always go back to Laragh, though I don't think she'll be troubled now by the person she dislikes and fears most. I imagine Fitz-Thomas has given up all hope in that quarter.'

'In every quarter,' observed Charleton.

'Yes. He gave up a lot a got very little in return. He is now in a state of complete dependence on your people.'

'And you may wish him joy of that!'

Charleton then met with his 'boatman' and a message

was sent by water to Tyrone House from where Gertrude's uncle, Mr Ffrench, would forward it to Laragh Castle asking his niece to come back to Galway to nurse the Governor. In his delirium Stubberd had been heard muttering about a 'long grey beard' but no one could make head or tail of what he meant.

In the meantime what would happen to the two young men in the citadel?

Charleton thought they would probably be held until the Governor's recovery. If that should prove to be slow it was possible that the recorder would decide what should be done, though, as Charleton said, there was no evidence to sustain a conviction in a civil court.

'Fitz-Thomas says these are the men he saw at the spot where he and the troopers were attacked,' Charleton told Dr Athy. 'But none of the others will identify them. And even Fitz-Thomas does not say they were armed. If right prevailed they would be freed, but they are guilty of being Irish and that might be enough to convict them.'

Indeed Fitz-Thomas's evidence of itself would not be sufficient to convict if the boys had not been Irish, for he had fallen very low in the estimation of those to whom he had sold his birthright. Most of them did not bother to conceal their contempt for him, espcially after his unseemly haste to indentify the prisoners as Tories. And now, as some of his former friends were quietly finding their way back into Galway not one among them would speak to or recognise the betrayer of the town. Distrusted by the Roundheads, hated by those whom he had betrayed and despised by all, he took to staying in the solitude of his own dreary home.

The Cromwellians of Galway had by now become divided into at least two parties. There were those who had early recognised that once Oliver's hand was no longer at the helm there would be a strong reaction in England, which in turn would affect the 'settlement' of Ireland. These were wise enough to adopt more lenient ways, in preparation for the coming changes.

Then there were the fanatics who were so committed to the policy of exterminating the Irish—for which they claimed they had a mandate in Holy Writ—that there was for them no turning back. They carried on, consequently, as if an Oliver would succeed an Oliver until the end of time, and they were thus quite blind not only to the general interest but even to their own.

This was the state of affairs when Gertrude left Laragh with many regrets to answer the call for her services to Colonel Stubberd. She had in mind, however, another and much humbler person who might need her help, the King's daughter who had endured so much.

She did not stay constantly in attendance upon the Governor as on the earlier occasion but called in reguarly to confer with Dr Athy and through her experience of his previous illness to give help and advice to those whose job it was to look after him.

Charleton was sometimes present during her calls but her attitude towards him was as if he were someone she had once met and almost forgotten. His determination to hold on to Lord Roche's lands was a barrier even to friendship, and she could not, or would not appreciate that his motive was to prevent Fitz-Thomas obtaining them. She recognised no motive which could justify a man of honour and integrity laying hold of anything under such circumstances: Acts of Parliament could not, in Gertrude's eyes, legalise a crime.

They met and spoke and parted like people determined to avoid controversy, but on one occasion she did remain for some time in his company. This was when he had some information about Carbra and Cahal which he was passing on to Dr Athy.

The recorder had sent them to Aran where they would be under the authority of the man who had arrested them. This was not too bad a fate, for that soldier, Buckley, was the man whom Gertrude had nursed through the plague some years ago, and he had not forgotten the kindness shown to him by the Irish then.

'There is a demand for labour to erect huts on Aran to house the various priests and monks who have been kept in jails all over the country,' Charleton told his listeners. 'I myself put it to the recorder that these two young men might be sent over there for that work. They will be better off there than in a prison cell, and in less danger of execution. But they must not try to escape another time. If they do I will not be answerable for them. Patience is their best chance. They way things are going they have a better hope now for justice, provided they don't spoil it by doing something rash.'

Should she tell Maeve, asked Gertrude, for she would be calling there as she did nearly every day. Both Charleton and Dr Athy thought that she should decide that for herself when she got there.

She preferred to go to the Claddagh by boat rather than by the West Bridge where she had to undergo the annoyance of being challenged and questioned by rowdy buffcoats. But as she could only do this at high tide she had to time her visits to suit the ebb and flow of the river.

There were always people in the little cabin where the King lay apparently oblivious to the talk and movement that was going on around him all day and half the night. It was a wonderful sight, so some thought, to see a grand lady from the *Gaillimh* side visiting the Claddagh. To be sure her visits were to the King's house, but all the same it was only a cabin like any other in the village.

But some of the older people did not like to see Gertrude coming. It was true that she had been very kind to Maeve, but it wasn't lucky, they thought, to have anything to do with the *Sasanach* old or new. Such were the mutterings of some neighbours whenever she entered the cabin, but though they gave her no smile of welcome they were not rude; just stolidly indifferent.

But Maeve herself made up for the chilling attitude of some of the Claddagh people. Her beautiful eyes lit up with their customary welcome as she ushered Gertrude in. Today she brought her into her own little room which was not much more than a shed behind the kitchen for Gertrude had news for her ears alone.

'Colonel Stubberd's illness,' Gertrude told her, 'has probably saved the lives of Cahal and Carbra. A good friend has stepped in and they have been sent to Aran, where they will certainly be safer.'

After they had talked for a little Gertrude went in to visit the King. The patient was lying in his usual fashion, in a kind of daze. Occasionally he would open his eyes languidly, then close them again on a world in which he had lost all interest.

NINETEEN

A Strange Ending

The Governor's recovery was slow despite Dr Athy's care. He was confined to his room for a long time, and he delayed his own convalescence by refusing to keep to the prescribed diet.

Charleton remained in constant attendance, and did his best to keep the patient within the doctor's limits, a good deed for which the self-indulgent Governor began to dislike him heartily. He was not surprised by this for he was also fully conscious of the fact that the men who had the most influence with Stubberd would do almost anything to get him out of the way. He would, indeed, have been happy to go, but for the problem of Lord Roche's lands, which he would not give up to Fitz-Thomas yet could not bring himself to retire to.

The fanatics' dislike for Charleton was aggravated by his outspokenness about political matters in England. It was well-known that Cromwell had already outlived his popularity there, and that his death would be hailed as a deliverance by many who had once supported him. But it was natural enough that the men who had fattened on his crimes and tyrannies should try to disguise that eventuality even from themselves.

At length, however, Cromwell died and on 15 September 1658 Richard Cromwell was proclaimed in Galway amid great rejoicings.

'Why do you rejoice?' Charleton asked the Governor and some of his associates. 'Is it because Oliver has gone to his reward, or because Richard has succeeded him? If the burden was becoming too great for the man of iron, what will it be to his wooden successor? I see no reason to rejoice, except for those who want the King's return.'

Some of his hearers persuaded themselves that Charleton was one of those who was at heart more Royalist than Republican. At one time their very suspicions would have been sufficient to hang him, but Charleton knew that there were others who thought as he did though they would not admit it yet. No apparent notice was taken of what he said, but later he found reason to think that his words had not been forgotten.

Illuminations were ordered in Galway, but it was noted that they were poor enough. People simply made a show of lighting up rather than risk the consequences. Even Mr Deane's house was badly lit; at least half his windows had not even a single candle, a fact which was noticed by people passing in the street outside.

'Candles are scarce enough in Deane's,' observed a buff-coat.

'I thought Deane was halfway to joining us,' said another.

'He will when he gets his daughter married,' said a man

muffled in a cloak.

'Oh, it's you Fitz-Thomas! It used to be said that you were keen to take her off his hands.'

Fitz-Thomas, still smarting from Gertrude's refusal, threw off an insulting remark about her which was heard by the crowd.

'Lynch Fitz-Thomas,' said a tall bystander, 'you shall answer for those words!'

Fitz-Thomas slunk away in the opposite direction while the crowd jeered at him, and for ten days after the incident he was not seen in the town, even after nightfall.

Then one morning when the Governor, at last able to resume duty, was at breakfast he heard a commotion on the landing outside. He sent someone to find out what was happening and was informed that a man was lying dead or badly injured at the foot of the stairs.

He went down to investigate, and discovered that the man was Lynch Fitz-Thomas. The sentry reported that this man had come in in a state of excitement and was about to rush up to the Governor's apartment. The sentry had told him to wait as the Governor was engaged, but he had brushed past him and started up the stairs. The sentry rushed after him with the result that he tripped and fell backwards, hitting his head violently on the flags.

He was not dead, but there was no doubt that he was seriously hurt. Dr Athy was sent for and reported that the unfortunate man had fractured his skull. He was carried to his own house, a cheerless place where he had spent scarcely a happy day in the past six or seven years.

Just before the doctor arrived a servant took a crumpled paper from Fitz-Thomas's hand which he gave to the Governor. It was only when Stubberd got back to his room after the accident that he looked at it, and then read and re-read it several times.

It was a letter addressed to Fitz-Thomas and signed by Rupert Charleton demanding a meeting to discuss the nature of Fitz-Thomas's remarks in public about 'a certain young lady'. Obviously the wretched man had read it and hurried directly to the Governor's house to ask his protection, but the very steps he had taken to save his worthless life had proved the short-cut to ending it.

Charleton was at Tirrelan at the time of Fitz-Thomas's ill-starred visit, but the Governor sent for him to come to town immediately.

'Did you write that?' demanded Stubberd, handing him the paper.

'Yes.'

'What did you mean to do?'

'To thrash the scoundrel within an inch of his life.'

'Well, you have been spared the trouble,' commented the Governor. 'What made you so angry with him?'

'On the night of the fifteenth I heard him using foul and slanderous language about a respected lady in the presence of a crowd of people, some of them rough soldiers.'

'Then it would have served him right,' said Stubberd.

*   *   *   *   *

So detested was Fitz-Thomas that no one could be found to nurse him or even attend on him but the old man and woman who had been his house servants for a time. None of his former Roundhead 'friends' would enter his house, for they despised him as someone who had taken his share of spoils which they had won in battle.

Fortunately he had in his enemy someone more generous than himself. Charleton hearing that he was thus shunned and neglected, went to Deane's and had a brief talk with Gertrude. Almost immediately afterwards she went with her maid to the house she had vowed never to enter.

Fitz-Thomas was in great pain but not delirious, and Gertrude saw that if anything was to be done it should be done at once, or he might drift into delirium or unconsciousness.

'Would you like to die as your people before you died?'

she asked him.

'What do you mean? he gasped.

'I mean, would you wish to die a Catholic?'

'Yes, but is it not too late?'

'Not too late for mercy. Would you like to see a priest?'

'But how? We banished them all—and I helped to do it!'

'You tried, but you failed. If you wish to see a priest one will come whatever the risk.'

Gertrude spoke a few words to Charleton who was waiting, and he immediately withdrew. She knelt with her maid beside the bed and prayed with the patient, and in a short time Father Anthony, dressed in his boatman's garb, came into the room.

'Now,' said Gertrude, 'here is the priest. We will leave you for a while.'

'Isn't that Charleton's boatman?' asked the sick man.

'Yes, but he is also a Dominican priest.'

Father Anthony bent over the patient and said quietly, 'My name is Anthony Browne and I was at school with you, but you wouldn't recognise me with the beard and in these clothes.' As he was speaking he drew out from an inner pocket an oilskin packet which contained his stole and breviary. Fitz-Thomas made a sign of assent and Gertrude and her maid left the room and stood at the window of the landing outside.

They were looking out in half-abstracted fashion at the crowds passing up and down when suddenly Gertrude noticed Jack Mathews coming towards the house with a huge book under his arm. If only Charleton were here! But he had gone to Dr Athy's for medicine for the patient, and there was no one to stop the Roundhead.

Mathews, accompanied by two soldiers, for he never stirred without his guard, was obviously coming to visit Fitz-Thomas. What were they to do? They could not interrupt Father Anthony and his penitent. They daren't let Mathews find the priest. In the midst of their dilemma the huge buff-coat was upon them, and Gertrude, trying vainly to stop him entering the room, found herself pushed roughly aside.

Mathews opened the door and looked in, then closed it. For a moment Gertrude hoped all was well, but he went only to summon his bodyguard, and the three of them rushed the dying man's room.

There was a lighted candle on the table and Father Anthony, wearing his stole, was administering the last rites.

'Seize him!' hissed Mathews. 'One of the Pope's pedlars here after all!'

As the astonished priest was seized, manacled and led out Gertrude and her maid moved to oppose the soldiers, but a look from the prisoner restrained them.

'What have you done?' said Mathews to Fitz-Thomas. 'I came to bring you salvation and I find you in the snares of idolatry.'

He sat down by the bed and began to turn over the leaves of his huge bible when suddenly the dying man, making a spring from the bed, flung himself upon Mathews and seized him with both hands round the throat. A soldier and the old servant freed Mathews with great difficulty and lifted the patient back on to the bed.

Then they turned to Mathews who lay gasping and threw cold water on his face. He opened his eyes and they helped him to his feet. Taking his bible he shuffled out of the room, but he had nothing more to fear from Lynch Fitz-Thomas. The unhappy creature was dead.

TWENTY

Doing the Work of the Lord!

Jack Mathews was himself again as he left the house with a

priest in manacles. He made for the Governor's residence and entered triumphantly.

'Another rat in the trap!' he exulted, as he recounted to Stubberd what had taken place in the dying Fitz-Thomas's room.

Then Father Anthony was led in, still wearing his stole.

'Behold, a Jesuit in disguise!' cried Mathews.

'Are you a Jesuit?' enquired Stubberd.

'I am not,' replied the priest.

'He is lying,' said Mathews, in horror.

'There is no need to rend your garments,' said Stubberd sardonically. He would not have been too much upset if the dying Fitz-Thomas had succeeded in his attempt to throttle Mathews. 'Is this not the man who passed as Charleton's boatman?'

'Yes, yes! Charleton has been in league with the Pope's pedlars. He is an even great sinner than they.'

The Governor gave orders to remove the prisoner to the West Bridge until the case could be more fully considered. Then to Mathews he said, 'I have some papers to attend to. You can look in again when Charleton comes.'

Left to himself Stubberd paced up and down the room muttering to himself. 'Lynch Fitz-Thomas, or Fitz-Judas as they called him, dead! If he had strangled the old Pharisee of Menlough I would have said he had done one good deed in his day. Mathews had been my evil genius. Even Coote laughs at me now, especially when times are so near a change.'

The sound of approaching footsteps chased him back to his desk and he busied himself with papers.

'You wished to see me, sir?' asked Charleton.

'It appears,' replied the Governor, putting down his pen, 'that you have been harbouring a Popish priest. You cannot be ignorant of the penalty for this?'

'Sir,' said Charleton, laying his hand on his sword-hilt, 'I am a soldier and have seen service as you well know. The person who makes any charge against me should feel quite sure that he can prove it. I have frequently employed to row me the man who saved my life. Unlike Jack Mathews I did not feel it necessary to enquire into the state of his soul. I took it that the soul of the man who could act so generously towards an enemy was in no worse state than my own.'

'Now, Charleton, don't be too confident. You are not out of the wood yet.'

He took a big official volume out of a cupboard and read from it a Parliamentary edict of 1649 which decreed that all who had served the Parliament of England in Ireland and had betrayed their trust should have their lands confiscated and their persons proceeded against by martial law.

'That is still the law,' said Stubberd. 'You have already had some trouble with your lands. . .'

'They shall trouble me no longer,' returned Charleton with spirit. 'Here,' he went on, taking a piece of paper from his pocket, 'here is my notice of surrender to those lands. You may forward that to the Lord-Deputy and Council in Dublin.'

The Governor read it with some astonishment, but he observed, I don't think this surrender will cancel the other penalties. Coote will be here soon. He is to become mayor on the twenty-ninth. I shall let the matter stand until then.'

Charleton went straight to Deane's to see Gertrude. He found her very upset, chiefly on account of Father Anthony, but also because of the awful death of Fitz-Thomas. She had some idea too of what might befall Charleton, but was relieved to hear that he had renounced his claim on the Munster estate.

'I had at one time,' he told her, 'looked forward to a different state of affairs. I had pictured a pleasant home on the banks of the Suir, with the charms of nature all around and the charms of a beautiful and accomplished wife within.'

Gertrude blushed, but she said nothing.

'All that is changed,' went on Charleton. 'I am almost certain to go to prison for a while. The only thing in my favour, and in Father Anthony's, is that the Governor and his colleagues do not all agree.'

'Don't say that you will be taken from us and that we shall lose our only protector!'

'You may take it as certain,' Charleton told her. 'I may not have the happiness of seeing you for a long time.'

'Oh, don't say that! I can't bear the thought.'

'I know you would not wish it, but I could cheerfully endure any bondage if at the end I could have the happiness of making you my wife.'

'But that is impossible,' said Gertrude.

'I know there is an obstacle. You think one religion enough for one house. So, it may happen that before I see you again you will be married.'

'I can promise you now that I shall not marry while you...'

Her words were lost in an uproar which had just broken out in the hallway. Two troopers burst into the room as Charleton demanded, 'What is the meaning of this?'

'Your pardon, Major. Our orders from the Governor are to arrest you and take you to the Lion's Tower.'

Charleton rose and gave his hand to Gertrude who clasped it in hers. Then it was snatched from her and manacled. As the prisoner was hurried out he heard a faint scream as she collapsed on the couch.

* * * * *

At Michaelmas, 1658, Sir Charles Coote was installed as mayor of Galway, with May and Ormsby as sheriffs, and Cuffe, recorder.

On the following day a special council meeting was held at which, among other matters, the charge against Charleton and the Dominican friar were discussed, Mathews surpassing himself in eloquence.

Coote yielded to no one present in ferocity, but he knew a little more of Irish history. He knew that new colonists had been forgiven and accepted among the Irish people if they were prepared to forgo their past oppression. He knew, too, that big changes were coming, and that his gigantic scheme of deportation, and the deliberate extermination of the Irish race, was far from completion.

Mathews urged that Father Anthony be hanged, and quoted an instance in Clonmel when a priest taken in the act of ministering to a dying man has been summarily executed.

'Clonmel!' cried Coote. 'That was the hottest piece of work Oliver encountered in Ireland. Men's minds were inflamed by what Clonmel cost us, and things were done which might not have been done later on.'

'Rebels ought to receive the same treatment at all times,' persisted Mathews.

'And ministering to the spiritual wants of a dying man is evidence of rebellion,' retorted Coote, glaring at the fanatic.

Mathews was so astonished that he sat down. Then recovering, he rose to attack Charleton. He cited occasions from the past when harbourers of priest were punished, but Coote interrupted him.

'Bear in mind, Mathews, that you are speaking to Coote, who is not ignorant of the work due to the Lord.'

After the meeting broke up Coote remained with Stubberd, discussing the impossibility of carrying out the Order in Council which had directed that the inmates of the jails be transported to the West Indies.

'I don't see how we can remove them all in less than two more years. Till then the priests in Aran and Bofin must stay there. Father Browne can go to Bofin and Charleton to Aran under the keeping of Buckley. I don't think we can court-martial him just now.'

'The treatment is mild enough,' commented Stubberd.

'Well, we must do the best we can. Our means is limited.'

It was not how Stubberd had heard Coote speak a few years earlier. Then the sole cause of centuries of trouble was the natives of Ireland. Sweep them out and replace them by God-fearing, law-abiding people from England and Scotland, and a reign of peace and brotherly love would follow.

Now this happy vision seemed to have vanished. And what would follow?

TWENTY-ONE

In the Home of St Enda

When Coote had ordered Charleton's banishment to Aran under the former Sergeant Buckley, now promoted Captain, he may have intended to humiliate him. But the new commander of the Aran Islands owed his promotion largely to Charleton and was consequently well disposed towards him. Nor had he forgotten that he owed his life to the kind citizens of Galway.

Meanwhile Father Anthony had been sent to Bofin. But in a few weeks he and a number of other prisoners were transferred to Aranmore, so that in a very short time Charleton and his 'boatman' were together again.

The prisoners in each convict station were dependent upon the attitude of the local commander and in this respect Charleton and Father Anthony were fortunate. Buckley was a humane man and allowed them certain privileges, such as the freedom to meet and talk together, and to move fairly freely around the island, and to mix with the other prisoners who included, of course, Carbra Conneely and Cahal MacRigh.

In addition, Buckley passed on to Charleton whatever news he himself obtained, so that fairly soon the prisoners knew, as did those in Galway who were not blinded by fanaticism, that Cromwellian rule was crumbling.

Charleton was not surprised by this news. He had been expecting it for some time, and on the whole he was glad to be detained on Aran and thus well away from the pettiness and turmoil which characterised the last stages of Puritan rule in Galway.

The question which had absorbed him from the beginning of his exile in Aran had nothing to do with the business of rising to power. It was a much more important question, namely, whether he should become a Catholic.

It was not a new question for Charleton. He had often touched upon it, somewhat lightly, in his conversations with his 'boatman' as they rowed up and down Galway Bay. But since they had come together on the island they had had the opportunity to examine it more profoundly, and to consider at length all that it involved.

Charleton had eventually narrowed it down to the issue of motive. Had he come to consider taking this important step out of genuine conviction, or was it simply that he wanted to marry Gertrude?

It would be true to say that he had begun to feel leanings towards Catholicism soon after he had arrived in Ireland. There seemed, however, to his way of thinking, formidable difficulties, but these began to disperse as his understanding of it grew. At length he asked Father Anthony to offer his own analysis of the motives affecting his decision.

'Put it this way,' said Father Anthony. 'Suppose you heard that Gertrude was dead. Would you still wish to become a Catholic.'

Charleton agreed that he would.

Some months before he was free to leave Aran he was received into the Church at the place where St Enda had preached, his sponsors in Baptism being Carbra Conneely and Captain Buckley's wife.

Thus were the feverish labours of Coote and Mathews and the rest of them gradually undone.

TWENTY-TWO

Jack Mathews has a Dream

But although the times were indeed changing Hardiman, the historian of Galway, relates that towards the very end of the Cromwellian domination there was a fresh—and as it turned out, a last—outburst of fanaticism.

'On 7th August,' he writes, 'an order was issued to apprehend Lord Clanrickarde, Sir Richard Blake, and other principal gentlemen of the country; and on the 22nd the (acting) Governor, Colonel Thomas Sadleir, was ordered to remove "all the Irish Papists" out of the town and liberties, and not permit them to return without licence from the commander of the forces.'

Some time later, on 29 September 1659, John Mathews was installed as mayor of Galway for the coming year, and it would have seemed that with his new honour and the order to clear the town he had much to rejoice about.

In fact, however, Mathews found a great deal to trouble his spirit. The new clearance order either could not or would not be put into effect. The property owners in the town did not want to have to take on, yet again, the care and maintenance of empty houses. And it was of no use the zealous mayor exhorting his citizens to 'carry out the Lord's work'.

Some months after the order was issued he called on Stubberd in tones of deep foreboding confided in him, 'I have had a dream.'

'Rubbish!' said Stubberd.

'Haven't you heard of Pharaoh? He had dreams.'

'Well what is all this gloomy talk leading up to?'

'This morning,' related Mathews, 'I carried my bible out on to the river terrace at Menlough as I always do on fine mornings, and sat down to read. I had read only a few verses when I fell into a deep sleep; and I thought I saw a great crowd of idolators carrying out their religious practices under my very eyes.

'Then I thought I saw Oliver standing there in his wrath. He unsheathed his sword and cut down some of these wicked people. Then he raised aloft the Book, but before I could speak I thought his foot slipped in their blood and the more he struggled to rise the more he became covered in blood. And there was great laughing and merriment among a vast multitude of these people.

'I woke up shivering although it was warm and sunny there at the time, and I was very troubled as to what the dream could mean. Camell persuaded me that it meant nothing in particular, but I can't help remembering Pharaoh.'

Stubberd tried to make light of the matter, though he felt somewhat perplexed and he wished fervently that Jack Mathews would dream happier dreams. Just then the new recorder of Galway came into the room and Stubberd suggested, 'Perhaps Edward Eyre can interpret your dream, Jack.'

But Eyre dismissed Mathews' trouble. 'Dreams are for leisure,' he said flatly. 'We have much more to worry about in George Monk. His march into England will do the Commonwealth no good. Lord Fairfax and the Presbyterians have gone over to the Royalist side. The Independents are outnumbered and Lambert's army is melting away. The fleet and the army are in Monk's hands, and they say he is negotiating with the exiles at Breda.'

'Nonsense,' exclaimed Stubberd impatiently. 'That is a very foolish way to talk.'

'It will do no good, sir,' replied Eyre, 'to blink at facts. Even in Oliver's day we were losing the power we once enjoyed, though you yourself would have hanged anyone who said so.'

'You have been plain spoken enough yourself at times,

Edward Eyre,' retorted Stubberd. 'And it has been said that you gave shelter to some of these idolators when the new 'clearing' order came out last autumn.'

'If Edward Eyre and his friends have interfered in the Lord's work it is no wonder we are getting evil tidings,' put in Mathews.

'Let me tell you, Mathews,' responded Eyre firmly, 'that there has been too much of this practice of trying to make the Lord a partner when doing the Devil's work.'

'And so what remains for Mathews and me?' asked Stubberd hesitantly.

'Very likely what happened when Oliver went to Drogheda,' retorted Eyre and he walked out.

TWENTY-THREE

Belshazzar's Feast

Stubberd had done very well out of his business association with Stephen Deane, the tobacco merchant. It suited him, therefore, to treat the news from England as misleading or exaggerated, and to maintain that things would still turn out successfully for himself and his friends.

A few nights after Mathews had told him his dream, Stubberd and the merchant were engaged, as they so often were, in discussing financial affairs. The subject of immediate interest was the cargo of tobacco now on its way to Galway. If it arrived safely in port the profits would be unusually high, and both he and Deane were considering the prospect of retiring and settling down on estates in a fertile portion of Clare-Galway. The area was one which had been reserved for 'the State'. In reality that meant for those people who, in Cromwell's service, had done especial wrong to the State.

'I think we would do well, Stephen,' he said, 'to retire from this hurly-burly as soon as we can pocket the proceeds of this shipment.'

Deane agreed.

'I have a bad reputation here in Galway, Stephen,' he went on, 'and I would like to move to some quieter place. Not that you have reason to complain of me. I have stood between you and harm. I could have exiled you; I could have even found ways to hang you. But I was wise enough to spare the goose that lays the golden egg. You may say it was for my own gain, and that is true. But it was for something more; it was for my happiness as well.'

Stubberd was leading up to a matter he had once hinted at, and which, though he had not mentioned it for over seven years, was still in his mind. He wished to marry Gertrude. He could not, he told Deane, openly defy the law, but a private marriage could be made acceptable in time!

Deane was speechless. He was well aware that Stubberd had no very strong religious convictions, and would quite readily conform to any form of worship so long as it advanced his prospects. But he also knew that his daughter would totally reject such an alliance, even if it were to cost her her life.

'If it had not been for me, Stephen,' Stubberd was saying, 'you might be a slave in the West Indies at this moment. You might remind her of that, and use your influence with her on my behalf. Now I am going to give her a present which I think will be worthy of her acceptance.'

He went to a cabinet and unlocking it brought out an object carefully wrapped in embroidered silk.

'Here,' he said unwrapping it, 'is a cup worthy of an empress. Look! It is encrusted with jewels. What's the matter?' he continued. 'You look anything but pleased.'

'A chalice!' exclaimed Deane in horror.

'I'm going to drink her health from it.'

'Do you know, sir, what you are holding,' asked Deane

urgently.

'I know it is an article of great value,' replied Stubberd, turning it round in his hands, 'and I would not part with it lightly. It was found with other spoils in one of the old Popish chapels. It is fit to drink your daughter's health in.'

'I can't stand by and look at this!' said Deane, making for the door as Stubberd set the chalice on the table to fill it.

At that instant the door was flung open, and a pale-faced man rushed past Deane and took hold of the chalice just as Stubberd lifted a flagon to pour wine into it.

'Stop!' commanded the stranger, removing the vessel.

'Who are you who dares to take such liberties with a colonel of the Commonwealth army?'

'I am a member of the Augustinian Order to whom this chalice belongs.'

'Deane, summon the guard!' cried Stubberd, excitedly. The next moment he had collapsed on the floor.

Deane did not summon the guard but instead helped the stranger to lift Stubberd on to a couch where he lay looking much as he had when getting over his attacks of the horrors on previous occasions.

Suddenly a great deal of noise was heard, in the house, on the stairs, in the hall and even out on the streets. A soldier entered and announced, 'A messenger from Dublin to see you, sir. He says he has a despatch which he must put into your own hands.'

A mud-spattered horseman entered and handed a packet to the haggard Stubberd. He had read only a few lines of the despatch when he let the paper fall to the floor and looked as if he were about to collapse again.

'That ruffian, George Monk!' he moaned. 'He has done it! Charles Stuart the Younger has been proclaimed as Charles II at Whitehall. There is a king again at Whitehall. At White-hall! At Whitehall!' He repeated the words several times looking as though he had seen a ghost.

A dozen or so leading Roundheads began to make their

way into his room. The messenger was recalled, and the account he gave of how the news had been received in Dublin and in all the towns on his way to Galway caused them the utmost dismay.

Stubberd whispered to Deane, 'Help me out, Stephen. I feel ill.'

Unnoticed by his perturbed colleagues Stubberd slipped out by a private way with Deane, while the Augustinian had disappeared in the commotion.

The streets which an hour earlier had been deserted were now filled with people cheering and shouting, 'Long live the King! Down with the regicides!' Even the soldiers were affected and cries of 'God save the King!' sounded from the barracks.

'I must leave, Stephen,' said Stubberd feverishly. 'I cannot remain here to be torn to pieces. See me safely out of town, Stephen!'

Deane was dismayed, but he could not refuse. They moved cautiously into the street but Stubberd was instantly recognised and surrounded by a crowd. There were some calls for a rope, but on the suggestion of a quiet-spoken man Stubberd was locked up for the night in the convent from which he had himself expelled the nuns. And there, in the gloom and solitude, the former Governor had time to reflect on how quickly a man's fortunes may change.

At daybread a voice broke in on his sombre thoughts.

'The blood of Charles I cries out for vengeance. Charles II would give something for the head of the man who beheaded his father.'

Stubberd rose with a shriek to find Deane and another man standing before him.

'Did you betray me, Stephen?' he gasped.

'No, he did not,' responded the pale-faced man who had removed the chalice some hours earlier. 'I saw you strike that blow; I have a relic of the occasion. We have come to put you aboard a ship that will take you out of here.'

Through a narrow door in the oak-panelling they led him down some steps, along a passage and up a ladder which brought them out on to the street. The passage, which had originally led to the church, was the same one through which Gertrude had brought Maeve and the other Claddagh women imprisoned in the old convent after the raid on their village eight years ago.

The streets were empty at this early hour except for the sentinel at the New Strand Gate who let them pass, and soon they were in a boat rowed by Deane and the Augustinian, with Stubberd crouching in the bottom as if afraid the very sea-birds might recognise him.

'That morning we met outside your house,' said the Augustinian to Stubberd, 'you recognised the beard I wore. It was very like the one worn by the man who cut off Charles Stuart's head. Wasn't it?'

Stubberd's only reply was to tremble violently.

They reached the skiff in the Roads and helped Stubberd aboard. He turned as if to speak to Deane, and the Augustinian showed him a blood-stained handkerchief, the souvenir he had referred to of Charles's execution. The sight of it seemed to finish him completely, and he fell senseless on the deck.

'I think I've seen you around the Governor's house recently,' observed Deane to his companion as they rowed back towards Claddagh.

'Yes. I had been searching for the chalice for a long time and I found out by chance that it was somewhere in his possession. I also had a strong suspicion as to the identity of the man who wore the long grey beard on the scaffold in Whitehall.'

TWENTY-FOUR

The King comes by his own again

It was almost daylight when they pulled their boat in to the
Claddagh, but the two men sat on in it talking for another
half hour. Not a human being was to be seen, even on the
town walls. The sea-birds kept up a noisy chorus as they
hovered and dipped in search of prey, and the rushing
waters of the Corrib grew noisier as the tide lowered, but of
other sounds there were none, and the two men remained
undisturbed.

At length the pale-faced man stepped out of the boat.

'As early as it is,' he said, 'I think they will forgive us,'
and he knocked on the door of the King of Claddagh's
cabin.

After a short delay it was opened by an anxious-looking
girl who fixed large dark eyes on the stranger.

'God save all here,' he said in Irish.

'God save you kindly,' she replied.

'This is the house of Conor Mac-an-Righ I believe?'

'It is.'

'I came to see him. . .'

'But he is ill. . .'

'That's Diarmuid's voice,' came a cry from the King's
room.

Maeve, who had supposed her long lost brother dead for
years was astounded and frightened, but to the old man the
voice of the never-forgotten eldest child was the cure he
needed.

He was out of bed and in the kitchen before Maeve had
recovered her self-possession, and as if by common impulse
all three knelt down and said a prayer of thanksgiving.

'If only the other boys were here now,' said the King, 'I could be perfectly happy.'

'They will come very soon,' said Diarmuid.

'They are dead,' said the King in great sorrow, believing that Diarmuid knew nothing of their fate.

'Not they,' replied Diarmuid. 'I saw them a few days ago. They are in the best of health.'

The King was incredulous. They had kept the news of the boy's varying fortunes from him for so long because he was ill that now they could hardly convince him of the real facts.

'They may be here by nightfall. The news was sent to Cashla yesterday, and it will go on by boat to the governor of Aran.'

'But what about yourself, my boy?' asked the King. 'How comes it that you are here now and that you did not come before?'

Diarmuid related how in a moment of boyish bravado he had gone on board a trading vessel which had been wrecked in the Bay of Biscay. He was picked up by a London-bound vessel with two other survivors, one of whom was an Augustinian priest who had been in Galway. He took Diarmuid in hand and got him an education, and in time Diarmuid had become an Augustinian brother. They were together in the crowd at Whitehall who had witnessed the execution of Charles I, and Diarmuid had dipped a linen handkerchief in the King's blood.

Some years later on his deathbed the friar had charged Diarmuid to take the handkerchief to the Abbey at Cong, and he had come back to Ireland to carry out this task. He had found a temporary refuge on the lovely island of Inchagohill in Upper Corrib, and had come into Galway in disguise from time to time. There were reasons why he had been unable to visit home earlier, and he did not wish to let the family know his whereabouts until he was free to come.

*   *   *   *   *

100

That night there was a gala assembled in the grounds of Menlough.

Jack Mathews had decamped. Earlier in the day he had been travelling in his barge from Menlough Castle to the town when he heard shouting and cheering for the new King Charles. Prudently he had ordered the barge to turn back to his estate and from there he beat a hasty retreat overland from the scene of his former power and glory.

It was the first happy gathering at Menlough for eight weary, blood-curdling years and Carbra Conneely and Cahal MacRigh were home in time to join in the tremendous rejoicings.

From a boat on the river Major Charleton, Father Anthony and the King of Claddagh enjoyed the scene.

On the following St John's Eve another great festival with a bonfire was held in the Claddagh.

The villagers in holiday attire gathered at the head of the village and were marshalled by the King into a procession which walked to the ruins of St Mary's-on-the-Hill. There on the site of the high altar stood Father Anthony and two other Dominicans in their robes. The King led Maeve out to where Carbra was waiting and they were married. Gertrude acted as her bridesmaid, to give herself courage, so she said, for another wedding soon to take place.

Mr Deane, meanwhile, had made sufficient money to buy a fine estate in County Galway to which he retired. When he died some years later he left this property to Gertrude and her husband, the former Major Charleton. The new occupiers of this land were so well liked and respected that even when persecution broke out again later they were left undisturbed, and so were able to give shelter and protection to others less fortunate than themselves.

MORE MERCIER BESTSELLERS

KNOCKNAGOW

Charles J. Kickham. *Abridged by Maureen Donegan*

Knocknagow is one of the greatest, if not the greatest of all Irish novels. It is a gentle and deeply moving story of rural life in a small village and is a classic of Irish literature. Generations have enjoyed the story of Mat the Trasher and Bessie; of the beloved Norah Lahy and lively Billy Heffernan; of the kindly Kearney family and the comic Barney.

But underlying the life of this community the dark presence of 'landlordism' remained a constant and brooding threat. We feel the passions and enthusiasms that swayed the peoples' hearts and we experience the atmosphere of the time, with all its hopes and despairs, hatreds and violences caused by evictions, starvation and emigration. Kickham's village is the soul and spirit of the nation and the charm and humanity of the people of Knocknagow remain eternal.

THE WILD ROSE OF LOUGH GILL

Patrick G. Smyth. *Abridged by Maureen Donegan*

The Wild Rose of Lough Gill, one of the most popular novels ever published in Ireland, is a colourful narrative written about the Confederate Wars. It is a fast-moving, romantic story of love and hate, war and kidnapping, cities besieged and gory battles with Cromwell stalking the land.

Edmund the hero involved in the Rebellion and his attempts to rescue Kathleen, the Wild Rose, from enemy hands is the central theme of the book. We see all the great historic events from their point of view and discover what effect the fall of governments, new laws and treaties had on their lives.

Seldom has a romance of such breathless excitement been combined with such a realistic picture of the times. This intriguing story ends shortly after the fall of Galway and the scene is set partly in Co. Sligo (near Lough Gill).

A SWORDSMAN OF THE BRIGADE

Micheal O hAnnrachain. *Abridged by Una Morrissy*

On a wild January night in 1703 a little lugger slipped out from the Kerry coast under cover of darkness towards France. Aboard her was young Piaras Gras with a group of fellow Irishmen leaving their conquered homeland to join the renowned and dashing Irish Brigade.

Piaras knew that the dangers and escapades of a soldier's life lay ahead. But not even his wildest imaginings could have foreseen the adventures which would carry him through the battlefields of Europe, up into a sinister fortress in the Alps and home to Ireland in disguise to recruit for the celebrated Brigade.

A Swordsman of the Brigade is an exciting and stirring romantic story, of the exploits of 'The Wild Geese' in Sheldon's division of the Irish Brigade in the service of France.

'.... the best present you can give to any person is a copy of this romance – you can steal a read of it yourself first'. – *Thomas MacDonagh*